MAISI

RELUCTANT ASSASSIN

MARTIN WALKER

This paperback first edition published June 2023 in Great Britain by Amazon.

ISBN 979-8-3976-1596-9

Copyright © Martin Walker 2023

The right of Martin Walker to be identified as the author of this work has been asserted by him in accordance with the Copyright, Designs and Patents Act 1988

All rights reserved. No part of this publication may be reproduced, stored in a retrieval system, or transmitted, in any form, or by any means (electronic, mechanical, photocopying, recording or otherwise) without prior written permission of the author.

This book is a work of fiction. Names, characters, places, and incidents are either the product of the author's imagination or are used fictionally, and any resemblance to actual persons, living or dead, business establishments, events, or locales is entirely coincidental.

1 - The Job

Well, I don't know about your average teenager, but my day started with the usual preparations for a 'dispatch'. That is - the death of someone.

It has descended into the predictable chaos my adopted mother, Olga Gabrys, creates from shooting some twisted scumbag diplomat in the chest with an AK-47 she picked up off the internet. She makes such an unnecessary mess, leaving *me* to clear up. Fortunately, I have learned how to efficiently mop up copious amounts of blood and other organs, disposing of them via any available means. Not your usual college day, I guess.

I, somehow, somewhere, missed the usual teen life with boys, Tik Tok and other addictions and exchanged them for bullets and fast food on the run (not on the go). Mind you, it has its benefits.

I know how to fight and subdue most brutes single handed, trained by Olga's martial arts obsession. It's always useful in case anything goes wrong with an operation, which it invariably does. I have broken endless bones, bashed people and prepared them for the afterlife (if there is one). Never killed anyone myself, though, leaving my mom to do the deed.

"That's my job, not one for you," she would say, her accent betraying her Lithuanian heritage. "I provide the money for our lifestyle; you are my sweep, watcher of my back."

Sure, I get involved but rarely do I get to pull the trigger. She sees me as an insurance policy, a backstop to any unforeseen event. Shooting off hundreds of rounds into fake men pointing painted guns at me is the closest I've come so far and is a fantastic way to spend my weekends.

"Come on, shoot harder and faster," she would yell. "You know our lives could depend on your accuracy, and you have to protect your mother!"

I nod as I put my eye to the sight for the fifth time. Yeah, protect her, that's the real reason behind this. If I had a normal life then I wouldn't need to worry about getting shot to bits myself, only on some gaming machine at worst. I always point true and firmly, blasting the heads off the effigies eager to greet more steel. Olga gloats over my accuracy and blatant determination to please her.

"Well done darling! That's my girl," she shouts in ecstasy.

I'm sure she gets more than a buzz from seeing guns firing off. It's more like spiritual, perhaps even carnal, seeing her shake with glee when a victim falls at her feet dead, unresponsive. Does she see in me a mirror image of what she wants to see? Another Olga, another dealer of death to people who have stepped over the line of decency?

So far, she has protected me from that role, for which I'm grateful. It is not something I really enjoy or desire. A job is a job, I guess. Some deal death in more subtle ways by restricting funds to health services, manipulating bank accounts, starving people of much needed investments to create a better environment. It all leads there eventually, but these people never see the justice they deserve. Hence, enter my mother, Olga.

Trained in espionage since she was a teenager, she works for anyone who gives her a decent return. Fluent in five languages, she is intelligent and attractive. At five feet nine inches, she is muscular and physically fit. A scar runs across her right eyebrow, which she hides with copious amounts of makeup so as not to detract from her seductive smile. Her mahogany brown hair shows signs of greying, probably due to her scary and exhausting occupation. Again, this is usually hidden with a suitable wig or hair dye. Only I know her real hair colour. Her hazel eyes are sharp and piercing, narrowing to slits when she is in death mode, but can be playful and full of mischief when she relaxes.

A resourceful woman she always completed a job to the end. At the buffet table, she waits for no one, gathering up the choicest morsel, along with whichever male is unfortunate enough to fall into her grasp. You could say man eater. More like male exterminator! Chew them up and swallow; they are never likely to see the light of day again! I'm sure that one day she will meet her nemesis and then she'll be toast. Until then, times are good. Money flows, along with blood spilled, so I can't be anxious about life. It's all I've ever known.

"You were the apple of my eye. You were alone and helpless, so I applied for your adoption and have never looked back," she keeps telling me.

Apparently born of British parents, they left me for no obvious reason at an orphanage in Lithuania. This is where Olga first found me when I was five. I have vague flashbacks which make no sense to me along with the snippets she fed me with over the years. I'm glad she did take me out of that place though. From what I've seen, I didn't want to be brought up with a load of disenfranchised kids, with an uncertain future. Although, the line of work in which Olga and I are employed, cannot be described as certain and stable. I suppose it's the calculated risk anyone takes with employment. Except - any mistake makes ours *deadly*.

"Maisie," Olga calls. "Please clean this AK-47."

"Yes, mother..." Always ready to clear up ...

2 - The Breakfast

"Pass me the salt, darling." Her voice is smooth and subtle. I pass the condiment without looking at her. We are in a boutique hotel in the snazzy part of Paris, the French police sirens occasionally whisking past the ornate frontage. Olga gives a glance to see if they are stopping outside and when all is clear she gives a silent exhale of breath in relief.

I smile to myself as I watch the nervous twitch which betrays her fear of being caught. The corner of her left eye slightly raises and then flickers until her heightened state of awareness diminishes. Her eyes darken then crease into that confident smile she so adeptly uses to ensnare her victims.

"Are we staying in Paris for long, mum?" I hope we are.

"Well... as always, it depends on..." she replies, raising her nervous eyebrow.

"On what?"

"I have a few things to attend to here, so, if all goes well, then we should have at least a few days. Why do you ask?" I sense her x-ray vision scanning my intentions.

"I would like to do a bit of shopping - never had time before just to wander," I answer, hoping that doesn't send her into a merry spin. Both her eyebrows lift.

Taking a fork, she delicately slices into the avocado and stabs at the smoked salmon. Here we go - a lesson on keeping a low profile. Slowly chewing, she lifts her eyes and lowers her brows simultaneously.

"I have no worries about you doing that as long as you …"

"… Keep a low profile, I know…" I say, giving that exasperated look of a teenager which infuriates her. She smiles, the corner of her mouth turning crooked.

"You have learnt that is best… for both of us, yes?"

"Yep. I'm not likely to bump into anyone we've dispatched, am I?" She likes this terminology rather than killing people, as it has a postal ring to it - sending someone from one place to another destination sounds poetic.

"Yes, that is true, but there are so many others who would like to catch us out… those who are in the same business…" She grimaces as if a hurtful thought invades her mind.

"Yeah … yeah - they are always on the lookout, I get it. I am pretty good at disguising myself. You taught me well, remember?" Tilting my head, I give her a knowing look.

"OK, if you promise not to wander too far and keep in crowded areas." She nods with her own instructions. I nod in reply. The omelette I ordered finally turns up on a blue and white Spode patterned plate with a delicate salad and baguette. Using this distraction, I stoke myself up to ask the awkward question I was intending. I feel myself squirm on the leather seat.

"You know that boy I met last time we were here … well… I'd like to catch up with him again if that's ok." A look of disdain flashes across her face, the one that makes my heart flutter with anxiety.

Olga has relationships with men all over the world, but for whatever reason wants me to keep all male interest at arm's length. Doesn't she realise I'm getting old; I need a boyfriend before it's too late! Sipping her Arabica coffee she brings everywhere with us, her face screws up. Sucking in the aroma she places the cup carefully in its saucer.

"Hmm… have you contacted him already? That is something I have always told you is dangerous. If you alert anyone where we are in advance, it can compromise our position." Shaking my head, I know it does and I have *never* done it. I'm not stupid!

"No mother, I am as careful as you - mainly…"

Uncontrollably I shake my head again. I knew this would be a pain. Olga's control over me is essential as I would be a great asset for anyone who wants revenge on her, a bargaining chip to turn herself in. But, with all the years I have followed her around and trained, *surely,* she would trust me to be watchful? Mothers! Is it the same for all teenagers wanting to spread their wings and break free from the claws of home?

Ripping the omelette apart in annoyance, I push it in my mouth. The baguette is the next victim on my plate as I tear it in half, dunking into the flowing egg yolk. Olga stares at my uncouthness. It makes me smirk, as warm yellow dribbles down my chin. Her turn to shake her head.

Distracted, her mobile phone vibrates on the table, and she swiftly answers it. Her eyes begin to twinkle. Is it one of her suitors or work? She says very little and gives a silly laugh. It must be one of her lovers. She never laughs if it's work. That is serious stuff. Anyway, that usually comes via clandestine means - a voicemail; a letter through the post; an email; a text. She has often picked up a library book and sifted through the pages to find a hidden code. The instructions once came by carrier pigeon, which was bizarre.

Olga hates birds as they freak her out by flapping around too much, so to receive her orders this way was hilarious. The bird was well trained to arrive outside our lodge in Romania and landed on the window ledge calm as anything. Until Olga got near it. Then all hell broke loose. Flying around the lounge, it would not perch long enough for her to make a grab. Feathers and crap went spraying everywhere. I had to come to the rescue once again and threw a blanket over it to retrieve the message tied to its leg. Unfortunately for the bird, I was too aggressive with the blanket.

It had a quiet ceremony in the backyard.

Placing her phone on its front she smirks with a mischievous thought. Winking at her, I hope to get more empathy for my own romantic intentions. It was wasted, though, as she cast her gaze towards a couple walking into the breakfast lounge.

A small blonde-haired lady, elegantly dressed in a neon pink ruched satin number, swaggered in ensuring all who watched saw how deliciously it hugged her rear. Behind her followed a taller dark-haired man with an open Armani jacket and trousers. Both drew unnecessary attention from Olga and many of the other residents. I watched as Olga's eyes morphed from a cheery girlish wistful look to the sharp steely awareness that I've so often seen before a knife or other weapon is employed to 'dispatch' the next parcel. I kick her under the table. In a whispered tone I ask what's wrong. She barely glances at me as she fumbles with her phone.

"I'm afraid breakfast is over. We must make a move - *now!*" I stare at her, then at the pair of models. What is wrong? They just look like a couple on their honeymoon or on a saucy weekend away. I press her harder for an answer.

"What the hell is wrong with you? I haven't had my drink yet. *Or* my fruit!" Olga always insists I have fruit at breakfast - good for the gut she instructs. I'm worried when the colour drains from her face. She hasn't been this agitated since a Russian spy, Dimitrios, betrayed her a few years ago when a hit went horribly wrong.

He was supposed to be collaborating with her to send a rogue CIA agent to 'sleep', but he turned on her. Cornered in a dark burlesque bar in Germany, a knife was being thrust towards her jugular. It was only by chance I had come down from our room to get a packet of crisps when I saw her in trouble.

At once my training took over. Taking a large bottle off the bar, I smashed it, creating a jagged edge just long enough to force through his trousers and into his femoral artery. He screamed in agony and fortunately twisted away from her neck. This gave her enough time to finish off the job and dispatch him to FSB heaven.

Lifting her handbag from the third unused chair at our table, she motioned to me to move quickly. I glance across at the couple who appeared completely oblivious of us or anyone else, now playing with each other's hair in that loved up way.

Frowning, I think this was Olga being over reactive. Or was it someone she knew? An old flame? Ex-lover? Or more sinister, a fellow assassin? These people do pop up at times and we must scram - double hits have occasionally collided and can be very awkward. I prod her with my elbow. She at last looks away long enough to catch my eye.

"It's not safe here Maisie - we have to leave." I keep on frowning.

"Yeah - I get that, but why? Who are those people?" I persist.

Ignoring me, she abruptly gets up and I follow as we march across towards the exit from the breakfast area. Standing momentarily under the sculptured archway, Olga glances back. She has now swung into operative mode. Carefully she moves her phone to take a picture of the unknown couple. Thinking she was at a safe distance and under the cover of a large-leaved pot plant, she snaps away on her zoom lens. I stand behind and to one side, peering through the plant to see if the couple are noticing this charade.

It could be seen as almost comical, the two of us hiding behind a huge plant pot. I have seen too many spoof spy movies where they act ridiculously in situations like this and ending up getting caught and then sent through idiotic torture scenes, eventually rescued by a chiselled featured male. A long and happy life to live thereafter. It never seems to play out like that for us. Reality is never as romantic as fantasy.

Content that she has enough digital evidence of them, we turn to run upstairs to our room. Hurrying along the corridor, I grasp her arm, this time with the intention of stopping her for some answers. Olga halts by our hotel door scanning with the key card.

"Inside - *quickly*." I have no choice but to skate into the room. Door shut; I try again to get her to look at me. Considering she is smoulderingly fit with rock steady nerves, her breathing is way more erratic than normal. Someone has really rattled her cage.

"Right - let's pack and go." Her face was a picture of uncompromised determination. The lines across her forehead seem to sink deeper the more she collects and shoves into her bags.

"Mum - I'm not doing anything until you tell me who they bloody well are!" I stand with arms wrapped around my chest, squishing my boobs. I give as hard a stare as possible. Collapsing onto the high double bed she sits, the slightest quiver releasing a tear down her cheek.

"I'm afraid my past has caught up with me…" she said, her normally resolute eyes dissolving into a teary wash. "That couple who walked in are the most adept assassin couple I have come across. They mop up others' failed attempts and ..." she stumbles as more tears roll. "... they end the careers of the assassins who are no longer required or are 'persona non grata'."

I look at her with disbelief. Sitting down beside her, I put my hands on hers trying to grasp what she is meaning. My mother - no longer needed? It can't be true. She has the most successful record of 'dispatching' compared to any of her contemporaries. A bit messy and untidy but I do my best to clean up, so it is untraceable, and a job well done.

A pang of uncertainty rips through my heart. What is the path of an unwanted killer except - to be *killed*? I shudder at the thought. Mustering up some encouragement I hold her by both shoulders and look her squarely in the face.

"Hey, are you sure mum? Do you want me to check? I can take a trip down to the reception desk and get the info on who they are." I am rather good at distracting and hacking into hotel tech. It's often the way we find where our targets are staying and helps Olga prepare. She shakes her head, splashing tears on my arms.

"No, I don't want you to get into harm's way. This is more serious than you know. When it gets to this point, it's like - there is no place to go…" Her painful expression spoke like an obituary.

An overwhelming feeling of dread sits on my chest, and I fill up. Trying to pull my emotions together, I race through a plan in my head but a knock at the door startles us both. Who is this? I look wildly at Olga who is already racing across the room to where she keeps her concealed weapon of choice.

The MC2c Mossberg compact 9mm handgun has been her companion since I could spit out my dummy. Lightweight and accurate, it's Olga's preferred self-defence weapon. Checking the magazine was fully loaded, she nods to me. I know it's time to adopt a defensive approach.

I carefully sidle to my bag as Olga skirts around a small table to get a clear view of the door. Picking up a surveillance wire with a camera at the end, I gently slide it through the gap underneath the door. It's a clever piece of tech as I can see the video on my watch and instantly get a picture of what and who.

Gently now, I don't want whoever is there seeing this wiggling wire tempting them to blast the door down. Twisting it carefully I peer up the empty corridor and then up a trouser leg and behind that, silk covered legs - nice colour actually… a pinkish hue.

Adjusting the angle, I can see the man is holding something close to his body. Not sure what it is, but another subtle twist of the wire confirms their intentions. The woman holds a Glock 42 close to her leg, safety off. Always a great carry gun, so small and light it can easily fit in any pocket or handbag.

I turn to Olga who is kneeling on one knee ready to fire. I notice a difference in her face from normal. She would be set with a steely focus in these circumstances, but at this moment I see a terror creeping across her eyes, almost a resignation to an inevitable end. I nod my head in confirmation this is not room service.

Another knock on the door. What now? We can't have this standoff forever. I feel my brow furrowing with impatience as I stare at Olga. Mouthing '*what do you want to do?*' I wait for the reply. Olga shakes her head to escape her frozen mind. Cold tears jump from her cheeks.

As if she has awoken from a hazy dream, I watch her eyes focus and zero in on a plan. My heart flutters and my back tingles as I know we are about to spring into action.

3 - The Plan

Under every welcome mat of our hotel room, we have the foresight to place a pad of electronics. This has many features. One is to alert us of anyone approaching the door if we are asleep and will wake us. Another is to fire a shock of enough volts to kill a cow.

Olga nods and mouths towards the case of electronics we carry everywhere. I immediately reach across and reveal the control panel set into the lid. Withdrawing the wire, I now concentrate on charging the static pad. She nods when the green LED light blinks with readiness. I place my thumb over the scanner primed to discharge the command.

First, we hear crackles and a fizzing sound, followed quickly by a rising yell of pain as the voltage ramps up. A bang on the door signals that someone has collapsed on the other side. I punch the air and shout a silent '*YES!*'. Now we have the option of opening the door and risking the other assailant still being ok and a shootout. Olga doesn't hesitate.

Running across she squints through the spy hole. Nodding to me, she grasps the handle and quickly turns it, ducking down at the same time. Her firearm ready, she allows the victim to roll into the room. It's the man. So where is the woman? I instinctively drag the man into the room clearing the doorway. Olga glances up and down the empty and eerily quiet corridor. I check the man's pulse, making sure he wasn't going to surprise us by doing a vampire-rising-from-the-dead thing.

The woman has disappeared, no doubt spooked by the collapse of her lover-man. I look anxiously at Olga who now has retreated into the room, frantically gathering her bags. She motions to me to do the same. I respond and arrange all my stuff into the couple of cases and backpack I use for all my trips.

Travelling in a hurry is routine, making ourselves scarce after a hit. But this has a different edge to it. For once, *we are* the hit, the ones being dispatched. A well of fear is rising, making me misty eyed and unable to focus. An unbearable desire to scream races through my head.

What does this mean for us? Who do we trust? The agency? They are the ones who have always given Olga the marks and paid her well. So, was it them that turned the table on us? Or is it another organisation getting revenge for all the mayhem she has caused over the past decades? Questions I will quiz her with - but not now - we must leave - *quickly*!

"Make sure he is hidden from sight Maisie - we must ensure that no one links him to our room." I look at her with a frown, searching for some inspiration for what to do about it.

"Where do you want me to put him? In bed? In the bath?" No way was I undressing him.

She shrugged as if it didn't matter, as long as he wasn't found in *this* room. I consider another option. Scurrying over to the French doors, I open them looking down over the veranda. The rooms appeared to be zig zagged across the building so each sitting area was offset from the next level. I march back to the lifeless body and grab him by the shoulders. You may think that a smallish teenager wouldn't be strong enough to drag a dead weight around like a toy doll, but the weight training I do in the hotel gyms pays off. He is rather a drag though - Armani jackets don't slide that well over carpet.

Getting him to the veranda took forever (*thanks mum for your help!*). I look across at all the adjacent ones to check no one is out sunning themselves. The street below is busy with morning traffic and shoppers, unaware what is going on directly above their heads. Checking again, I haul him up and over the rail, his arms dangling. I set my sights on the next level of verandas and lift his legs, so the weight is now all on the top half of his limp body. It's a struggle. Out from a pocket a phone bounces onto the floor. Distracted by it, I let go - a bit too early and his feet suddenly disappear over the edge. Oops - I meant to be more angled so he would land a few floors down.

Peering over the rail I can see his disjointed body sprawled across the chairs of another veranda just below us. Grimacing, I study how he has finally settled. His head was wrenched back by the impact giving the impression he is taking in the morning sunshine. His arms are splayed outwards, his legs twisted in a weird tangle. However, he sits neatly on one of the chairs, so all things considered I shrug thinking it doesn't look too bad - for an accident. Olga takes up the electronic pad and discards the burnt mat in a cleaner's trolley.

"Come on - we don't know how long we have got before more arrive," she pants, beckoning me to move quicker.

More? How many are after us? I slip the phone in my backpack and scuttle along the corridor keeping a lookout for the woman and anyone else suspicious. We take the stairs as it will lead directly to the reception and a clear view of the main doors.

"Maisie, we will hail a cab and make for Charles de Gaulle airport. I have a plan to lay low in England until I figure out what is happening." Her eyes are wild as we clamber down the stairwell.

OK. I don't mind staying in England, my birthplace. I might persuade her to look up any family if I still have any there.

"Will we be in London or in the country?" A rather stupid question to ask as our asses are currently on the line. Olga ignores me.

We reach the last door on the ground floor. Carefully opening it, she furtively glances back and forth. Was the woman waiting? Were there any others joining? Mum did say there maybe. How are we going to blend in well enough to get a cab without alerting all the assassin world to our escape?

Olga nods indicating the coast seems clear. I stumble through the door far too loud, clattering my backpack against the elegant brass door handles. She shoots a death stare at me for being so clumsy. I smile sarcastically and try to remedy my accident by tiptoeing across the polished marble floor. The revolving door swivels welcoming our hasty retreat to the polluted Parisian morning air.

Cabs are waiting in a line sympathetic to our plans. Olga commands the first driver to load up quickly and I help with throwing our various cases into the boot. So far so good. We fall into the rear seats, with my heart rate reaching its upper limits for stress.

"Aéroport Charles de Gaulle dans la mesure du possible s'il vous plaît!" she reels off with ease.

I relax and fall against the headrest with sweaty brow and armpits. Phew, I must stink! When I get stressed, it seems all of hormone city breaks loose. Time for some deodorant. Reaching into my backpack I fumble about for my spray. Instead, my fingers grasp the phone I idly placed in there earlier.

Pulling it out, I wave it in Olga's face. She screws up her nose and then realises what I have. Smiling, she takes it off me, as I look back at a commotion in the front foyer. Police have just arrived, probably alerted by someone finding a stranger admiring the view from their veranda without permission.

As they pour through the revolving door, a familiar dress appears on the sidewalk. Those stockings do clash with that neon pink dress come to think of it. I nudge Olga who acts instinctively to protect me and pulls me down. Her hand is already fixed to her gun now waving it at the driver to get going - *vite!* He pulls off narrowly missing an oncoming police vehicle. The sound of a crack reverberates off the cab boot lid.

Was that a shot? I stare back at the woman who abandoned her lover and take in as many of her features as possible. The long blonde hair is floating around her square chin, dark slit eyes staring back at mine. A chill runs down my back activating the cold sweat on my t-shirt. Olga sighs with relief. I am hoping she still has a plan to escape and work out who and why *we* are the targets.

4 - The Airport

My mind is awash with conspiracy theories as we wind through the Parisian streets. If this is an agency directed commission, then we are stuffed. They have all manner of nasty people they can draw from to turn us into dust. Olga seems less interested in any theory as she is staring at the phone.

"Can you hack into this Maisie? It would have been far easier to get his finger to open it."

I smile and rummage around in a side pocket of my pack. Something I always carry around is a forensics kit to extract fingerprints, usually for cloning, to pin others at the scene of a crime we commit. I study a film I pull out and carefully take the phone off her.

Placing it on my knee, I wrap the phone in it. Pressing my hot hands over it, I watch as the prints appear on the underside. Now it's a matter of finding the correct one. Blowing on the film to set them, I systematically try each one. It takes time, but I find it. The screen bursts into life.

A pretty woman adorns the profile picture - not the one that shot at us. So, she was obviously *not* his love interest. Olga snatches it back and scrolls through the texts for any clues. It seems there is only one - she shows it to me. I suddenly feel faint, and my vision goes woozy. Am I really seeing this?

"It seems that I was not the target, dear ... it was *you*!" Olga states. This is what I am trying to push out of my head. The target is *me*? What the hell for? I'm not the assassin.

"Why ... *why me*?" I stutter as I fall back heavily, sinking into the seat as far as I can. Olga curls her bottom lip over in thought. My head is spinning with a weird sensation, and I feel a swell of sickness coming up.

Gagging, I wind the window down urgently and puke up all over the side of the taxi door. The driver shouts something I can't hear as the breeze is wafting his words away, along with my omelette. Olga pats my back in that patronising way to try and calm me down. Wiping my mouth, I regain some focus again and grimace at her. She smiles trying to show me some empathy - after all, it's usually *her* that is the focus of any heat.

"Well ... that's interesting."

"*What*? Interesting .... is that right? I call it bullshit!" Anger is growing with my feeling of indignation. "I don't get it. *Me*? ... Surely, you're the obvious choice... sorry." I squint at Olga's concerned expression. Nodding, she seems to agree.

She flicks through the phone screens to find anything else to give a clue. The last phone number appears to bring life to her twitching eyebrow. She looks up and stares vacantly. I nudge her for an answer. Blinking as if she has come back into the cab again, her face creases and that crooked smile flickers.

"There are certain things that can race up behind and bite you when you least expect it. This I feel is one of them." I stare at her. What is in my past that is coming up to bite *my* butt? I think she needs to explain. "I have always protected you from harm …" at this comment I cough - yeah, a life following an assassin is keeping me from harm.

"If you say so," I reply sarcastically. "So, what do these people want to *bite* me for?"

Her face can morph so easily to hide her true intentions to maximum effect when duping weak men and self-assured women. All except for me - I know when she is trying to avoid telling me the truth. This was one of those faces, eyes shrinking to slits and her face slightly colouring up. Licking her glossy lips, her gaze drifts off to the side window.

"Some things in your past are racing up to catch you I'm afraid. I have been able to hold back the tide but maybe it's time to get away from the tsunami that is coming." I'm frowning so much it hurts my face as she attempts this poetic analysis of our predicament. *What the f...?*

"What are you on about Olga?" I call her by her name as this is freaking me out. Am I the adult in this relationship? This sounds more than just a guess - she knows more. She looks down at the phone. The number flashes up again, causing a grimace to creep across her face. "What's that number? Who does it belong to?" Come on mum, you know.

"A long time ago I accepted a job which made me sick at the thought, but it was a necessary one, saving a greater catastrophe - all for the greater good you might say."

My curiosity piques as the car swings around into the departure drop off point, so distracts her from continuing. We must unload. The driver is wary of Olga who has been waving her handgun around like a lit cigarette, so sits perfectly still until we extract all our luggage. He screeches off, I guess to down a bottle of vodka, and thank God he is still in one piece.

The airport is busy, as we push through the bustling crowds. In our hurry, I didn't see Olga book any tickets so I'm not sure how this is going to play out. We head for a desk that has few people around it. It doesn't have any of the main airplane company logos but one I have seen before when we have flown in a hurry.

The Phoenix Flights Airway has a fleet of five Cirrus Vision SF50 planes based at different airports around the world and are unbelievably available for us each time we need to escape quickly. It allows us to travel freely without all the usual checks. She nods at the lady at the desk and presents her phone, displaying a code like those you get on any Amazon packages but with greater complexity for security. The scanner flashes green accepting her code and the tickets are printed.

We walk through the airport to a secure lounge area, with a man offering us a cool drink and hand cloth at the door. Olga accepts the offer; I smile and pass - I need a coke and head for the refrigerated can dispenser.

Dumping our bags by the reclining seats, we look through the viewing window as we drink our cool liquids through dry lips. I turn to quiz her again about this '*sick*' job she had to do. "Well … what was this job mum? It sounds fascinating." She glances around ensuring no one is within listening distance.

"I will tell you more when we are airborne. You will have to realise that I had no choice in the matter. I was young and ambitious. No job seemed to be too difficult, and the payoff was oh, so tempting. I was up for anything. My judgement was not as refined as it is now…" I allow myself to laugh thinking that she must have been crazy reckless then. I often wonder about her current capacity for stupidity.

"Well… go on then!" I sound impatient because I am - it's my life that appears to be snuffed out. I need an explanation. Her crooked smile comes and goes like a tormented faulty light. Clearly, she has difficulty in telling me any information about this and I am far from relaxed. Rocking about on my heels I slurp more coke as I stare blankly out the window.

"Before I tell you anymore, I want you to promise me something…" Oh yeah - I can sense one of those get out of jail-free-card things about to be played. "… don't fly off the handle. You must be prepared for some serious revelations about my life and … yours."

Well, that's reassuring Olga. I thought it was all going to be a big mistake - a misunderstanding, one which we can patch up over a few drinks. This is really freaking me out now. I pivot on my heel and see that there is no one other than us in the lounge. Where have all the rest gone? I nudge her, and she turns. Her face drains once again. I fear that we have not missed our flight but our advantage.

A man stands at the door and closes it, giving us that menacing look of imminent doom. I gulp as coke fizzes back up my throat and nose, making me want to cough. Olga stands square on to him drawing composure from who knows where. We have no electronics to zap him. No surprise tactic. This could be messy.

5 - The Fight and Flight

At first, we just stare at him, a lean man who wears his clothes as if he had fallen out of a charity shop after trying on every random combination. Jeans with rips across the knees, a loose hanging t-shirt with a zombie picture scrawled across the front, his face is covered with dark stubble and bits of white around the mouth. Perhaps he had been eating some ice cream and forgot to wipe his lips? A weird looking black trilby hat with a white band sat cocked to one side. Does he model himself after Michael Jackson? Maybe I'm just making too many connections here - MJ - zombies …

I shake myself from the fantasy and see a knife appear from his hand previously concealed along his wrist. Seriously - you are going to attack us with a *knife?* Who do you think we are? Some fresh tourists you can screw over by terrorising us?

Then, without any warning, he flings the dagger straight at Olga with such speed we both struggle to react. It catches her in the shoulder and pins her against the wall. She lets out a scream sending a shock to my belly. I glance across to check that it's not life threatening and launch myself towards a nearby chair grabbing the arms, tossing it as hard as I can. Another knife rips through the fabric seat as it clatters in front of the man, who is now throwing more knives like confetti. Bloody hell, this guy must be from a circus. I upturn a table and hide for a moment trying to figure out what to do.

Olga has forced herself to hide as well, edging towards our bags. I never carry a gun but now wished I did. The only possible weapon I can use is my wit. The man advances thinking we are on the defensive and I agree. On my leg I carry a wire to which is attached a small but very sharp blade. The wire is designed to rip through fabric and when tightened around a neck, will garrotte someone with ease. This has been a recent addition to my person as anything else is too bulky and obtrusive.

Quickly I unwind it from its housing, deciding how to attack. He is breathing down my neck as I dive across the polished floor and slither on my side. I flick the wire, directing the blade at his legs. It slashes his left leg and causes him to falter, the clatter of knives bouncing on the floor. His yell is somewhat overstated to say he is some sort of paid killer. Ridiculous!

I keep the momentum and fling it out again this time at his torso. The rip in his shirt now matches the ones in his jeans except blood pours from it making it look more zombie-like than ever. He staggers to one side as he tries to draw another dagger from his jeans. Then, a crack explodes above my head and the man's forehead punctures with purple and black, throwing him backwards over the jumble of furniture. Olga stands holding her trusty handgun, blood running down her white top. Her hand quivers a fraction. This has shaken her to the core.

"Are you ok mum? I need to check that wound."

I search around in my backpack for something suitable to stem the blood flow. A small hand towel will do for now. It's manageable, just a mess. I glance into her eyes. The look of resolve is fading as the loss of blood and pain kicks in, the adrenaline overriding her senses.

"It doesn't look too bad mum - we can cope with this on the plane." I try to reassure her and smile. She returns a weak crooked one.

"Yes … Come on, we must move." She drifts a little and blinks trying to get focused.

I gather all the bags, giving zombie-MJ the finger as we head for the stairway leading to the plane, glancing around to make sure no more surprises are waiting. It's a difficult descent as I'm trying to steady Olga and carry all these bags. If we had only known what today was bringing, we would have travelled far lighter.

The walk across the runway gives me the shivers as we are in the open and anyone can pick us off, so I hurry her along at the risk of increasing her pain. The steps are down inviting us to board although a flash of mistrust enters my subconscious.

What if this is what they want? Get trapped on a plane with no escape? NO! I shake it out. I know that Olga has trained me not to trust many people, but I can't afford to descend into neurosis. We will never find a safe place with that sort of thinking. Hauling her up the steps, she stumbles through the doorway. A concerned flight attendant reaches out a hand, frowning when she spots the blood-soaked towel.

"It's ok... my mum has had an accident and I will sort it out when we are airborne," I say with more authority than usual and she nods, helping us with the bags.

I guide Olga to a waiting cream leather seat. That's not a good colour for bloody clothes. She collapses, relief running across her weary eyes. I instruct the flight attendant to hurry the pilot to leave as soon as possible, after asking for a first aid kit. The wound is clean but deep. I swab away the dried blood and any bits of her clothing embedded and then clean with a washwipe. I carefully place the hydrocolloid gauze and secure it.

"I don't know how many times I have had to save your ass mum, but this is going to be in the top five," I say with a grin, finally relaxing a little.

She looks around for the drink's cabinet. I suspect the pain is more than she's letting on, so a bottle of rum will satisfy her needs. She chills as the liquid slides down her eager throat with ease. Wiping her lips, she blinks, and a gentle rest falls over her eyes.

"Better?" I ask.

"Yes Maisie, much better. You are so good; I have taught you well." She hesitates as she wants to say something else, but a stab of pain cuts across her face again.

Is it the shoulder or a deeper wound that she was about to reveal to me earlier? I rest back in the opposite chair. The seatbelt sign flashes up. Finally - taking off. The flight attendant is attentive and then returns to her station and belts up. I feel pressure forcing me back in my seat. The plane's motion means that we will get to safety soon.

Olga smiles a little - the rum is having its pleasing effect. Personally, I have never liked alcohol much - probably seen too many people acting recklessly and stupidly around her which has made me wary of it. I prefer to be in control of everything, the opposite of my mum, who too easily descends into chaos. I must be her levelling influence, which is why she considers me her talisman, her guardian angel.

"Maisie," she starts to speak slowly and measuredly, for her. "It is time I was… straight with you about some things. As I have said… my aim was to protect you from harm. Part of that was to ensure you could survive in this crazy world of espionage and 'dispatching'.

You have seen many disturbing events… and had to cover up my failings at times…" Too many, I think.

".... but with all this comes at a price to me - and to you. The agency has always been a stable and trustworthy employer. But there was one truth I always hid from them and … you." Her face grimaces. The plane levels off and we can release the belts. I move to the edge of my seat. What's this revelation? I am intrigued now, a worm dangling on a hook.

"My motivation for getting this work was a mixture of hate and greed. My family were decent and hardworking, my brothers and sisters' good upright citizens." I didn't know she had any other family.

"Over time as the west was eroding the Russian Soviet Union, Lithuania regained its independence in 1990 and I was born into great celebrations. However, there were elements of the old guard not wanting this transition and began a series of underground cells who would act out the will of the newly formed FSB in Russia. In 1999 I was in the middle of a family party waiting like everyone for the countdown to the new century. I was ten years old." I saw her face replay a painful episode.

It was one I had never watched before, her expression betraying a hidden past. A tear formed in the corner of her eye. She twinged and touched her shoulder.

Another drink is needed, I think, and pour her another. Her eyes glaze over.

"I can see the laughter and joking; the fireworks crackling over our heads, sparklers and drinks fizzing. My father lifted me up to see the rockets exploding with blues, greens and reds flashing across the dark sky. It was a celebration of escaping tyranny and hope for the next generation to enjoy the freedoms of another century.

My mother Natasha was dancing with my sisters, and everything was wonderful. I didn't know at the time that my father had been part of a resistance group fighting the Russian authorities for years. It seemed that all was now well, a peaceful life for us Lithuanians." She downs another shot of rum. Choking, she allows a sob to escape. I reach out and hold her hand tightly.

"Hey, it's ok. I never knew any of this mum." I am dreading where this story was going. "It sounded like a lovely time…" Composing herself she smiles weakly.

"It was. Until I watched in slow motion as at first my mother was shot in the head, her warm blood spraying across my face. Then one by one, my brothers and sisters were mercilessly killed. My father ran with me into the house hiding me in a secret place and told me to stay still and quiet. He smiled and blew me a kiss, replacing the false door. I never saw him again. All I heard were the cracks of Kalashnikovs and people screaming shielded by the fireworks. I stayed there for hours not moving, frozen in fear and sobbing quietly."

I feel my eyes filling up.

A warm sensation rises through my body as I see the picture of little Olga traumatised and lonely in this hideaway. I can't contain my own sorrow. Any of *my* memories before being adopted by Olga are lost in a fog. We both weep quietly.

***

The plane bounces through turbulence as we descend into London City Airport, our silent vigil maintained for the last half hour as I take in the details of Olga's life after surviving the family's slaughter. She was found a day later by her uncle and aunt, taken into their family, and raised as a resistance fighter herself. Even though there was little need for this as Lithuania was peaceful on the surface, her uncle was determined to find who had attacked the family.

Olga had suffered so much sorrow early on in her life that I could see that it had hardened her heart and sent her on a personal mission of revenge and hate. She explained how as a teenager herself she was approached by a secretive agency who was hiring young ambitious talent for their operations. She grasped at the chance, expecting to embed herself in this clandestine world of assassins and hoping it would lead to her family's murderers.

"Did you find them?" I ask as we hit the runway with a bounce. She nods. "Oh … good; I expect you got the revenge you wanted." A shake of her head signalled regret.

"Not exactly. Time had moved on and these people had also moved on. They were now respectable people, with their own families and happy lives. They were not involved in this dark world any longer, the one I had fallen into. At first, I had so much hate, so much pent-up rage because these people had robbed me of a happy life. Then I watched through my scope as young brothers and sisters were running and laughing, a pang in my heart made me stumble; was this going to satisfy my empty cavern of bitterness?"

"So… did you dispatch them in the end?" I could see the struggle in her face.

"I had come to the end of my trail. What was I to do? Let them live their wonderful life or inflict what I had to endure? I was paid to execute a job, a hit; professional duties had to take over. I pulled the trigger and watched blood spatter the children's faces. I died a second time even though I continued firing, one by one falling around the screaming kids. It was not the redemption I was seeking." Wow, my mother has a sea of emotions I never knew about.

Our heart to heart is interrupted by the flight attendant opening the door and lowering the steps. Impatience overtakes me at the interruption, and I give her a hard stare. She obviously gets the message and retreats into her safe zone by the kitchen area acting scared for some reason. I am not normally scary, only when my teen rage erupts over the lack of food or sleep. Neither of these are in progress, only curiosity and this precious connection with my mum. I don't want to lose it. Olga nods to me to leave, even so.

We descend the steps; I help Olga as she gingerly climbs down. A car is parked nearby, and a man stands beside it. He beckons us over.

"Did you order a car to pick us up mum?" I ask suspiciously. Olga nods but looks uneasy about it. "Are you sure? You don't think this is another trap?" I sense a tidal wave of mistrust growing in my chest. I am now thinking that even the flight attendant is going to leap off the plane and stab us with a pastry slice. Glancing around, no one else is hovering, except this bloke, who is smiling rather too much.

"Welcome to England. My name is Gustav. I am your chauffeur for the day. May I take all your luggage?" His well-spoken English offers no reference to a possible

Swedish background, so I am curious why he has that name.

I only know about names originating from Scandinavia because I watched a film once about the assassination of a Swedish king, Gustav III. It was on TV in the hotel room while I was waiting for mum to arrive back after a lengthy session with one of her men. It was an old film from the seventies, not what I normally watch but it held some current interest for me. The king was killed by someone who betrayed him acting on behalf of a group of conspirators. This confirms to me I am already considering Gustav to be a modern-day conspirator - maybe the king has come back to wreak his revenge…

He offers a helping hand to alleviate my balancing act, taking the bags and placing them carefully in the boot. We settle onto the rear seat of the freshly valeted black BMW 3 Series sedan.

Soft music is filtering through the rear speakers, some sort of classical stuff. I would prefer a modern alternative; Mae Muller, Caitlyn Scarlett, or Madge but mum will probably appreciate this in her current state. The strange thing is, it brings a weird swell of emotion, which I can't account for or want. I have never entertained such music as it reminds me too much of psychopaths from films listening to opera as they plan their next devious kill. Am I becoming like that??

I feel her forehead as she's looking a bit pale. She may be running a fever, so I ask Gustav to take us to a pharmacist. He nods in the mirror and gently pulls away. I try to make Olga as comfortable as possible by placing the cushions around her. Still as independent as usual, I am brushed off like an irritating fly.

"Please don't fuss - I'm ok, just a little lightheaded." She gives me a concerned look as if I'm the one who should be watched over. "You should know we are heading for a safe house in the Peak District, one that I have had for many years." That's a place I have never heard her talk about before. So safe, even her own daughter knew nothing.

"Arr, ok… that seems good. I hope you have got some sort of idea for our future. If people are after us, we will have to plan very carefully." She nods in agreement. Sinking back into the soft seat, I am wondering what sort of future we *will* have.

6 - The Drive

The car glides along the motorway effortlessly and uninterrupted except for Gustav asking if we are ok and comfortable. I feel he is too interested in our wellbeing just for a chauffeur. His eyes are too close together and his smile reveals some greenery he should have brushed off before picking us up.

All things being equal (whatever that means), we are trying to be at ease with mum falling asleep several times, leaving me to stick headphones on and be the detached youth I would be in the real world. The on-board chocolates are welcome, and I munch through the whole box, feeling my waist grow exponentially (maybe too big a word, but it sounds like I feel).

England is pretty at this time of the year with the spring blossom bursting out all over. Flowers and trees seem to be celebrating the increased light and warmth with a kaleidoscope of colour. It ends up being a bit of a blur though as I keep drifting, unsure if I should keep my eyes open for anything that would take us by surprise.

Gustav pulls into a service station, explaining he needs a pee. Olga rouses and pulls a face as her shoulder reminds her that being awake is painful. Maybe we all need to pee, so I ask her too. Nodding, we wait until Gus, (I find myself giving him a nickname now), has returned and will wait for us.

The fresh breeze ruffles my long black hair, swishing around my face like a tormented ghost as we make our way to the loos. We don't often come to England but there is something comforting about it. The style of life is familiar even though I have never lived here (except for my first five years). Maybe some subliminal thing is going on that I don't recognise. Or maybe I am indoctrinated by too many TV shows and films I watch late into the night.

The loo stinks of ammonia and neither of us dawdle, choosing our own hand wash as we walk back to the car. I scan around the parking area and see a mixture of tourists, workmen and soldiers wandering between their vehicles and the shopping mall. It all seems quite innocuous and sublime - this escaping death. That is, until I spot something which anyone else might have ignored. Pulling in a few rows behind us slides in a black transit van, with shaded windows. I try to pick out the plates and immediately feel my anxiety spike. They are French.

"Mum… I think we had better get moving." She looks at me knowing that I am serious. Most of her training has been reconnaissance based and she has done a great job at passing that onto me.

"What have you seen? Are we in immediate danger? Make sure Gustav has the engine running," she says urgently.

We stride as quickly as we dare, without giving away we know that our position is compromised. Seeing Gus sitting at the wheel obediently like a well-trained spaniel dog, I wind my finger forward, hoping he gets it. He does and the engine fires up. We slide through the doors and tell him to shift A-SAP. He speeds away, nearly toppling people with their Costas over the faded pedestrian crossings. The speed ramps are raced over with no effort; we must have some sort of improved suspension.

I glare back to see if the vehicle has moved. It has! But I can't see it anywhere. I feel panic rising in my throat and try to cough it out. Quickly I scan around the parking area. *I can't see it.*

"Gustav please watch out for a black transit with French plates - I suspect it may be following us," I gasp.

He nods and races through the gears as if he can't decide which one to use but has the desired effect of getting us out of this place efficiently. At the junction to the motorway, again I look around. I didn't see it coming…

The van was speeding towards us from the right-hand side. Gus must have spotted it in time as he launched the car off at an angle, wheels spinning, causing the van to veer off into the other waiting cars. The noise was deafening, a mash up of metal and glass smashing around us. Olga has a gun in hand and has that look on her face which can only mean one thing. She wants blood.

A blur races before my eyes. Men in black (not the movie) jump out brandishing semi-automatics, their heads covered with balaclavas race towards the back of the car. How is it that everything slows down when danger is all around you? Olga opens her door and glides down so low only her head and upper torso hang out. She fires low too, aiming at the men's legs, I guess assuming they don't have bullet proof leggings on.

Well, it was a good hunch, as they tumbled one by one. The odd thing when slow motion takes over your worldview, your reactions don't speed up to take advantage of the surreal moment. I feel like I am encased in blancmange and feel utterly helpless and useless. Gus has not responded to it either. All I see is his twisted expression of *'what the hell have I got myself into'* look. I ignore his gormless expression and mouth 'get our asses out of here', also in slow motion, without the special effects of my voice sounding dull and low. It was more of a scream.

I grab Olga by the waistband, so she doesn't get spat out with the sudden spurt of speed. We indeed fly off. The boot gets rattled with a round of semi-automatic fire but thankfully doesn't penetrate the seats. I haul Olga back in and she swings the door shut.

We are now whizzing along the motorway so fast I'm worried that the police will be the next to tail us. Gus has gone into flight mode, swerving past all vehicles as if they are stationary. Olga breathes out heavily. Sweat is peppering her forehead. With her hair in disarray, she appears to have just left a sauna. My heart stops for a second. I see red oozing from a wound above her hairline.

"Mum! You've been hit." Stupid thing to say when I can see she knows.

I'm running out of small towels, so I use one of the cushions and place it on her head. Blinking again and again, Olga grimaces as this one is exceeding her general pain threshold and gives me a swipe. "Hey! Sorry..." I know she didn't mean to be so unappreciative.

"Maisie ... you would never be a great field medic - you lack the tender care required."

She takes over the pressure of my hand and steals a quick gin from her stash. I tell Gus to cool it and slow down - I doubt whether the van or the men would be in any fit state to follow us. Turning back to mum, I am full of questions.

"We have never been in this situation - you must have really pissed someone off - or *I* have. So, what is this mystery you have been trying to share over the last few hours? I think I need to know... at least before I have my head blown off." I cross my arms waiting for Olga to be in a more responsive mood. She gives me a side glance.

"When we pick up the hire car, I will tell you the rest. It's better if we are alone." She inclines her head towards Gus who has wide eyes staring on the road ahead. He must be thinking of joining the taxi driver in Paris for a drink and sedative… if he survives the next part of the journey.

7 - The House

The hire car is waiting at a garage just off the motorway and Gus is more than glad to get rid of his dangerous cargo - his expression is priceless. Eyes wide and flitting around; hugely different to the confident self-assured individual that met us in London. Bless him. Not the usual chauffeuring work, I guess. Handling the bags over to the SUV the sweat is pouring down his face as he stares at the bullet ridden boot. We say our farewells and thank him for being so brave. He nodded and said it was a pleasure. Somehow, I think he was lying …

I swear silently as I realise that the bags had taken the force of the bullets and probably made a cullender of my clothes. Oh well, we will have to go on a shopping spree when settled into our temporary home. Not that I can call any home permanent. We seem to move around from one hotel to another with such frequency that any time we have off from 'dispatching' is spent on a Greek island. Don't get me wrong, that is pretty idyllic, but sometimes it would be nice to have a place which is familiar and cosy.

Olga takes the keys and without thinking sits in the driver's seat and taps in the destination. I gaze at her through the window and shake my head.

"If you think I'm letting you drive, you are crazier than usual!" No way is she driving in this state. You might as well let the hitmen kill me!

I open the driver's door and tell her as firmly as I dare to get in the rear seat. It does cross my mind that maybe I should have taken my test, but I have driven so many vehicles illegally, another one will be fine. If I observe the law of the land, then there is no reason for any coppers to pull me over. Not like when I had to cross the Russian border once with Olga shouting at me to drive as fast as the army jeep would go. That was hairy.

***

Being chased by a group of drug laden thugs on motorbikes, firing at us was no fun. She had previously said 'farewell' to one of the drug barons within his millionaire mansion just outside St Petersburg. Nicely done, actually… for her. Poison was the method, efficient and clean. Not the usual mess I was used to.

However, we had not counted on his wife being so ruthless and cunning. Having been given the job by the agency, we didn't realise that it was *her* that had organised it. Death by proxy one could say. She was wanting the husband out of the way so she could make off with all his cash and shack up with her lover-man. The main reason for chasing us, I believe, was that she had watched how deliciously Olga had seduced her husband and perhaps a tinge of jealousy stabbed at her heart. We were quietly getting away with it until she sent a rain of thugs to chase us.

Driving the rough terrain towards the border was a challenge. We were bouncing around in the jeep like Mexican jumping beans (have you ever seen them - *weird*!). The GAZ Tigr I hijacked was amazing, handling like a tank over ditches and rocks without any problem. I left Olga to do the shooting as usual.

She was not dressed for the occasion, sporting a low-cut black chiffon number with heels which she was determined to keep on even though we were tossed around on a spin cycle. It gave her freedom, however, to manoeuvre herself into the perfect position to distract the following entourage by dangling her breasts. Then she let rip with the semi-automatic delivering more than an eyeful to those too close. What a star! Never fails to amaze me how low she will stoop.

This car, however, would not need the distraction of Olga's naked body to get us to safety. I will drive the remaining 50 miles north peacefully, hoping that no one has traced our movements and Olga can sleep easy. Glancing in the rear mirror, I see her stretched out and has already drifted off, clutching her shoulder.

A wry smile creases my face as I must admit, this life we lead is far from boring. I have seen so many places and encountered such a rich variety of people, that normal schooling would not touch five percent of.

I am so ready for some recuperation at this mystery safe house and planning our next moves. Until then, I must concentrate as my eyelids are heavy. It's ages since I've eaten any wholesome food and my stomach is growling. A coke which I snatched at the service station will have to feed my brain for the time being.

***

It's not too long and we are winding through some awesome countryside in which Olga called the Peak District, somewhere in the middle of England. Rolling hills and stone walling stretch for miles in all directions. Sheep and cattle are the only living things I have seen for hours now. The satnav is guiding me to our destination somewhere near Hope, which has a certain irony. I'm thinking that is what we need oceans of. The SUV makes light work of the steep hills and narrow rough roads, making navigation a doddle.

We pass a stately home on the way with wide open vistas to gaze upon its elegance and ornate architecture. Deer straddles the road slowing down my manic pace, along with my heart rate; I am almost feeling normal again. I haven't even glanced in my mirror to see if anyone is following us, I am that chilled.

Driving up an unmade track the satnav gives me the cheery announcement that we have arrived at our destination. I pull alongside a stone wall with a blue gate.

The name 'Blue Haven' dangles on a post next to the front door. Wow, this is what she has hidden from me all these years? This looks to be a perfect home for us. In the middle of nowhere, surrounded by stunning countryside. What's not to like? Then I ponder. Where are the shops and the night life, we are so accustomed to? Hmmm… maybe not that idyllic after all. Olga groans and opens sleepy eyes.

"Ah … we are here then? Well done, Maisie. Was it a good drive?" I nod and tell her about the number of times that sheep and deer tried to steer me off into the gutter.

She smiles a crooked smile and swings her legs out of the car. As she stands upright, I watch her face morph from dozy, to pleasure, to pain. Is it good for us to be here or not I wonder?

"I can't believe you have not told me about this place before. It's ace. Except I didn't see any McDonalds or night clubs nearby. Good job I have enough music to keep me happy. Have we got the internet here?" Olga groans and advances towards the front door.

She scouts around the porch looking for something. Then she prods the stonework. Is she checking that it's free from rot? "What are you doing mum?" I ask in my annoying tone.

"Looking for the key… it's here somewhere." She continues to press each stone around the left side of the door. One of them makes a popping sound and magically the door clicks open.

"There we are … it's so long ago I couldn't remember where it was." Obviously, mother, you are getting old and senile; easy to forget a hidden key in a stone wall. Fascinated by this tech built into the fabric of this old house, I study the stone she pushed. It appeared like all the rest, but on closer inspection I could see it was made of plastic with a lens underneath.

"Does this have a biometric fingerprint reader built into it?" I ask, now intrigued that we are entering a tech savvy Beatrix Potter house. She nods and staggers towards the kitchen area. "I will bring the bags in, ok? Is there any food here, cos' I'm dying from starvation?" My pleas fall like dead leaves as Olga is now out of ear shot, scuttling somewhere through the house. I unload the SUV and dump the bullet ridden bags in the hallway.

The floor is hard and grey presumably laid with flag stones from the local area. The stone walls are thick and chunky, ideal for keeping out the cold winters and any random bullets from our assassin friends. Pictures adorn the walls of flowers and animals, small pieces of pottery placed carefully on tables alongside an old chaise sofa. The colours are pastel and gentle, which is confusing me as this is not the usual taste of my flamboyant adopted mother.

It reminds me of those old movies where an old woman entices young innocent kids in to steal them from their parents. (I must stop watching ridiculous movies late into the night). I walk through into a spacious room with a low ceiling, filled with burgundy furniture and a huge stone fireplace. It's late now and the night sky is black and lightless. I am itching to start a fire as I can feel goose bumps on my arms and legs.

"Shall I get a fire going?" I ask as if I have done this all my life. To be honest, the only fires I have started are those which create a diversion away from our escape.

***

One was particularly explosive as we dispatched a local mafia schmuck in Sicily. Giorgio Tonelli was a nasty person dealing in the lives of refugees escaping the ravages of war and starvation, turning their lives into more misery with prostitution or as drug mules. The man shared his name with a philosopher apparently and could not be further away from being an altruistic person. His favourite pastime was separating the children from their parents and selling them to rich families around the world. Those that didn't comply, he would personally cut out their tongues and make their partners eat it. This was one man that I was happy to see dispatched.

Olga had infiltrated his inner circle with her usual wit and charm posing as a wealthy Russian who wanted a lovely young girl as an adopted daughter. At a dinner party on the island, we had been invited to attend a passing out parade of the children. It was like a bizarre talent show with the kids marching out in front of these 'inhuman' beings.

I sat alongside Olga seething with anger and wanted the whole sick event to stop. She, as always, waited for the right moment. Leaving me to set up the diversion, Olga charmed her way into Tonelli's arms, and they quietly retired to his bedroom. I didn't see what she did to him initially, but when his body tumbled from the balcony and dangled by his balls, I knew it was time for the real show to begin.

I had prepared a set of charges around the base of the luxurious mansion house where he lived, primed for Olga to make her exit. I wore my trusty black Teflon and Kevlar all in one jumpsuit for such occasions which I can keep hidden underneath any other clothing without being detected. The hoodie and pull up balaclava completed the set with electrostatic gloves and boots. A neat little number which I chose myself from the FSB sales in Russia.

Carefully I traversed the perimeter and laid the exit explosives to give us time to slip away with all the other scared 'guests'. The resulting explosion wrecked the foundations of his mansion and lit up the night sky as the whole edifice collapsed, much to my satisfaction. I was even happier when I watched the bus ship the kids to safety - a little touch of humanity which I organised with a local charity for abandoned children.

**

A quick strike of a travel flint and the fire bursts into life. For some reason I carry this around with me ever since watching Bear Grylls surviving on the open grasslands of an African country. Just in case, I like to be prepared – DYB-DYB, and all that. Olga reappears in a red silk negligee, which I am slightly surprised about as she was not in the mood for a relaxed lounge around the fire when we arrived. A bottle of gin is securely grasped in one hand and a folder in the other. She collapses in the seat nearest the fire and flings the file across to me.

"Have a read of that… it might shed some light on our predicament." Oh, ok Mumsie. What is this revelation going to be, I wonder? The brown folder has an inscription on it.

'CLASSIFIED - TROJAN HORSE'

Ooo, this is intriguing, although I thought it was a type of condom from what I heard.

Shuffling on my bum, I sit crossed legged and open it to reveal photos and memos. The pictures are a series of meetings, probably taken from a rooftop with a telephoto lens as they are grainy and in black and white.

The groups are of four or five people gathered around boxes and crates of what look like weapons. The same people seem to be present in each one, with two others.

The memos appear to be from MI6, the overseas British Intelligence Service, covering covert arms deals and plans for invasions of various countries. Up and down my back I feel static racing as it dawns on me that the UK seems to be involved in plots to destabilise these countries so that they would fall under the wing of NATO.

"This is deep shit!" I say that with stronger emotion than I expected.

Looking up at Olga I see her glazed expression slip away and she nods. I continue to take in the scenarios these documents spell out. **TROJAN HORSE** was organised to infiltrate the rank and file of the country's army and recruit factions to create the eventual internal breakdown of the command structure. I couldn't believe what I was reading. The UK involved in coups all over?

"How did you get hold of all of this?" I ask. This is not the usual stuff she handles. Not the assassination of a country's security services.

"It was my big break twelve years ago I was telling you about. The agency wanted to stop these plans from succeeding and the only way was to take out the chief architects of it. It was a bonus begging to be taken. I could have retired there and then; it was a huge pay out." I stare at her and wonder why she didn't. "Other things… persuaded me to carry on…" she continues, her crooked smile directed towards me for some reason. "As I said before, there are some things I never let the agency know… the truth has been released somehow, somewhere and I have to work out why and by who!" Her face screwed with annoyance and determination. It didn't answer the question about what it had to do with me though.

"So… what is the deal with me and these killers?" Olga glances away again and swigs a large gulp of gin. Wiping her mouth, she hesitated as she did before we got attacked.

"I hope you're going to tell me before another guy comes crashing through that door and blasts us to hell," I say, pursing my lips. I'm getting more agitated each time she avoids this part of the story. "Who or what is 'Trojan Horse'? Do you know these people? Are they the ones you killed?"

"Yes, they are. I had to track them down for months as they had extreme skills of avoidance." Hmm, like someone else…

"MI6 had given them so many false identities, my reconnaissance was getting more and more frustrating. The agency was not patient. I had to arrange to be a broker with the Ukrainian security services as a last resort which nearly compromised my position. They were suspicious of what was happening and an old friend from my early days of training got involved in the deal."

"So, you have always needed a guardian angel even before I was trained," I say with more than a little scorn. A wry smile creases her face, her eyes lighting up for a second.

"It seems so Maisie. I lured them into a trap where they were vulnerable to be picked off like a sweet strawberry. I was positioned 500m away with a Havak Pro Hunter rifle and 'dispatched' them when they were enjoying a river side break by the Venta River in my homeland. They were given the premise that a nice holiday would be a good idea after the deal was done."

Still, I'm wondering what this has to do with *me*. Especially as Olga now looks at me with gooey eyes. What the hell is wrong with her?

"Anyway, there was another problem which I had to cover up quickly and efficiently and hide from the agency," she says, her eyes slipping into sleep mode. She was drifting off to ga-ga land as the drink was having its effect. Great! I try to extract more, but she waves me away, saying the pain is too much.

It looks like another wait for the truth!!

8 - The Stranger

I cover Olga with a quilt from one of the bedrooms and leave her to dream down 'gin river' and go on a wander. I want to explore this fascinating house and find any more interesting features. The biometrics reader installed for the entry was a nifty piece of kit. Not only did it read a fingerprint, but it was also accompanied by a DNA sampler. I only found this out when I fiddled with it and a needle shot out and stabbed my bloody finger! Ouch! And it was bloody... all over my top.

Wrapping it up with a tissue, I went in search of some food. The kitchen was fully stocked with fruit and veg, and the fridge surprisingly was oozing with lots of goodies. Snatching a smoothie and a salami pizza, I continue to explore. It seemed to me that someone knew we were coming or someone else lived here. Why else would all this food be here? Strange. I don't remember Olga giving any advance warning.

The downstairs is laid out with three rooms all with ancient rugs and furniture, very unlike our usual hotel rooms. The paintings hanging on the stone walls depict landscapes and flowers. I was desperately trying to find any photos to get an idea who lived/lives here, but they were sadly lacking.

Each room has an open fireplace with a well-stocked basket of wood neatly chopped. I run my fingers across the tops of the leather and corduroy fabric musing who looked after this place and kept it so neat and tidy for a safe house. Drinking my smoothie, I come across a room with a bookcase stretching the width of the inside wall. Wow. Never seen so many books. I've learnt most of my stuff from Olga or the internet, so this was novel. Pardon the pun…

A wooden desk stretches out in front of it inviting me to sit like some professor. I obey and lean back on the chair which reclines with a squeak. Kicking off my Converse trainers, I put my feet on the green leather top and imagine I'm a clever old geezer about to interview some poor geek for a uni. job.

Leaning back, I gaze at the ceiling which has swirls and patterns, presumably in plaster. The lead glazed window looks out onto a large expanse of grass and then beyond that, farmland. Very relaxing.

My foot slips as I'm drifting off and I throw my hand out to stop me from falling to the stone floor. It's then I notice a small window on the desktop, only highlighted by my blood smeared mark.

"That's interesting… I wonder what that's for?" I didn't have long to wait. I nearly crap myself as the middle of the desk suddenly flips over revealing a computer screen. Blinds start to unravel from hidden compartments across the windows and the bookshelf begins groaning. I feel like I've been transported to a high-tech Indiana Jones movie. Behind me the once extensive bookshelf has disappeared by swivelling into wall cavities, revealing a steel door. My God what have I stumbled across now? I jump as the computer starts to speak.

"Welcome Maisie. It's been a long time. I hope you are well and safe. I am happy you have found refreshments and I am able to order anything else that is lacking. Please let me know." *What the hell?* A computer is talking to me as if we are best mates.

My mouth hangs open and I stare at the screen. There is no freaky avatar, just a speech wave. How does it know me? I try to mouth some words, but air just escapes my vacant expression. Clearing my throat, I shake my head.

"HOW do you know me? What … *What the hell are you?*"

"All relevant questions, I'm sure. It is a surprise for me too that you have arrived after all this time. Let me assist in showing you."

I stare as the screen flickers with images of people who I've never seen before. A couple and a baby along with a toddler. Pictures and videos of holiday times at the seaside, some I recognise such as Paris and the Caribbean. I move forward, continuing to suck on my smoothie, the montage demanding my attention.

It appears to be a timeline of whom, I have no idea. My mind is so confused I am trying to stop myself from glazing over. These places seem to strangely jolt a memory. The woman in the videos appears to like opera and sings at various concerts. So, is this their home? It would fit the profile of the twee furnishings and setting. One after another, concerts in Vienna, Copenhagen, Oslo, New York, Rome flash up across the screen.

Wow, this lady is good. Not that I like the music, I thought to myself. "She must be well known," I say out loud. I instantly wished I had kept quiet as the crazy computer started talking again.

"Yes, indeed she was. Many awards she won for her performances around the world. A renowned soprano singer: opera was her life." I am awake enough to realise this machine is talking about this person in the past tense. Do I ask? I know this thing has me hooked.

"Ok... who was she then? And dare I ask ... Do you have a name?" I feel I'm going to regret this.

"Her stage name was Maria Giogorgi - had quite the Italian flavour. She sang for over twenty years, mesmerizing audiences with her range." Yeah, a bit like now...

"As for myself, I am merely a computer-generated voice and have no specific name. You can call me whatever you like." This thing is asking for it...

"Ok... seeing that you act like some sort of butler, I'll call you ... Anton." *Why Anton? What is going through my head?*

"Perfect! It has a certain charm to it. I'm sure that it will be an acronym of some sort. I will consider it. It has a meaning of priceless, which is appealing." *Oh my God... this thing is getting all gooey about a name I've just dreamt up! Come on...*

"Well, while you consider that, why have you suddenly burst into life and started chatting to me like some long-lost friend? I've never been here before. Is this something that Olga has set up to make me feel at home?" *It doesn't respond as quickly, and I am wondering if it's gone into sleep mode or something.*

"You say Olga... that is, Olga Gabrys?" *I nod my head. Does it see me too?*

"I see ..." *What does it see?*

"I am Maisie Gabrys; you know *me* for some reason, so presumably you know *her*?"

It was silent again. I am feeling this is acting like Olga, avoiding my questions. Am I the only one who knows nothing? I bang the desktop trying to get it to respond. Maybe a foolish thing to do, as simultaneously the computer screen flips back into the desk and the bookcase returns to its original position with a crunch as my smoothie bottle is crushed in the gap.

I shake my head wondering if this ever happened - was I delirious or something? I mutter to myself and wander back through the house to stoke up the fire. Olga is snoring unashamedly, and drool is dripping down her chin. I mop it up and replace the duvet she has kicked off, tucking it under her. I stroll back to the kitchen now obsessed with finding out more about this opera singer, but food is still firmly on my mind, so I pull out a pre-cooked curry and bung it in the microwave.

"If this computer - or Anton, as it likes to be called now - knows about us coming here and actually knows who we are, why did it scurry away like a frightened mouse?" I am speaking out loud to check I am still awake and not dreaming. This house has more secrets than my mother. To be set up with such high tech, it must be an agency safe house. Or is it totally off grid, not even they know about it? I hear a whirring sound which freaks me out and I check around the kitchen for anything moving. *What's that?* I spot a camera in the top corner of the ceiling. Something is watching me!

"Oi! Whoever you are - *piss off!!*" A voice softly echoes around the central island.

"Sorry, I didn't mean to scare you. It is Anton. I was confirming you were alone."

"Bloody hell... are you a pervert as well? Why are you checking that?"

"My programming does not require me to have human frailties, so no, I'm not a pervert. When you said that Olga was here too, I had to check you were safe."

"I was *safe*? Why wouldn't I be? She is my mom. You really are crazy. Why all the secrecy?"

"It is part of my protocol to ensure your safety." I am stunned by what Anton says. It's programmed to keep me... *safe*?

"Don't you mean *the agency* keeps us safe?" This Anton is doing my head in.

"It would appear that certain truths have been buried and you are not up to speed. I shall have to consider what course to take over your education." *My education?* Now Anton wants to be my teacher!

"Well, while you *consider* that, I'm making a curry, so bog off and leave me in peace!"

Food is now my priority, but I am torn between quizzing him more and eating. However, today has been a such a whirl I need some space from any further surprises *or* 'education'. I turn back to the sizzling dish and breath in the sharp aroma and sigh.

9 - The Dress

The curry sits happily in my stuffed belly as I drink a glass of coke, pleased with myself that after a manic day, we at last have some relaxed downtime. It's late and the full moon casts its light creating a lattice pattern from the leaded windows stretched out across the floor. Olga has slept continuously leaving me to explore this house further. A loud belch spontaneously escapes as I climb the stairs. Weird, that taste which hitchhikes a belch. I'm not sure if the mixture of coke and curry is pleasant or not. Anyway, these creaky steps are always ready to give any intruder away - no need for an electronic pad in this place.

The landing stretches out to meet five doors, each painted with an olive green and fancy ceramic handle. My eyes follow an ivy pattern tracing its way around the walls linking the downstairs. The first door reveals a bedroom with double bed and wardrobes and French doors leading out onto a glass balcony.

I run my fingers along the soft silk sheets and wander across to the wardrobe. Inside a vanity light displays a dazzling array of colourful dresses, I guess for the soprano's performances. This woman must have been short, as I measure myself against a plum-coloured V-neck split front number. She must have been stunning in this. Taking it from the hanger, I drape it over me and gaze at myself in a full-length mirror, imagining I'm at the opera.

I let out a shrill note and wished I hadn't. That damn computer.

"You look good Maisie. A perfect fit. Try it on and you will be surprised." Like now - get out of my head Anton!

"You do realise that your presence is freaking me out. Is there anywhere in this place that you cannot see or comment on something? Can I switch you off like Alexa?" I wait for its reply, hoping I've shamed the unashamed machine into submission.

"Yes, of course. I cannot leave the property, but I can give you more privacy. Apologies. It is exciting to finally have you here. Although excitement is an emotional response to which I do not have. Just a figure of speech." I nod my head and give it the *'finger'* of speech. The light on the camera fades, at least giving me hope Anton is finally asleep like Olga.

I throw the dress onto the bed and gaze at the dressing table where jewellery is draped across a stand in the shape of a tree or deer antlers; they twinkle in the moonlight. Are they real diamonds and sapphires? My God these people are rich, man.

A necklace with a huge central sapphire, encrusted with diamonds forming a flower catches my eye. This has got to be tried on. Undoing the clasp, my fingers tremble as if I'm handling explosives. It sits perfectly around my neck. Tempted, I am going to try on the dress and get the max effect. No Anton to perve, so I can relax.

Slipping off my dirty and sweaty jeans and top, I slide into beauty. I never get a chance to glam up like this normally - only if the job demands it. The last time was a charity ball when Olga had to pose as a wealthy businesswoman; me as her secretary. A bit young for a PA but that's why I had to glam up. Makeup and the full works - made me look at least twenty-three. Why that age I don't know, just what I think I *would* look like!

***

We were both dressed in jade chiffon gowns and being a masked ball, we could have had any face but for close encounters Olga had to look right as she was banking on intimacy with the mark. This one was female - a right nasty bitch. Michela Dobrinsky controlled trafficking anything that she could make money out of. Drugs, people, data - she would be there.

Based on the shore of Lake Geneva Switzerland, she had the appearance of a humanitarian, but her seedy operations filtered into every corner of the world. The agency was clear on their demands for this dispatch. She had to be publicly humiliated at this ball and shown for what she really was. Dignitaries from all over the business world came together to celebrate the start of a new initiative. It was to create a network of data technology to reach into the poorest communities and bring much needed business investment. Behind the scenes she was manipulating the poor and hijacking the businesses for extortion and using these channels for her own illicit ideals.

I was given the task of hacking into the presentation and reveal footage of her dealings with drug barons and sex traders. Not an easy operation when security was run by her criminal gangs posing as respectable servants and admin staff. The data operations centre was cleverly hidden into the fabric of the mansion. I had researched on how to tap into the cables that powered the operation and so slipped away when Olga had Dobrinsky in her clutches.

The tech we have from the agency is so cool, I sometimes wonder if it's from another world. This nifty pack had nano-clips, when fixed to the power router sent messages to the central processors which returned the control to me. The problem was finding the right cables. Also, they were buried in concrete and stonework!

Another cool piece of kit! The glasses I wore could search through most materials like x-ray vision and pick out the trail of power. I had to be careful when to power them up as they only had fifteen minutes running time and the lenses glowed red; not a good look for a respectable secretary. Avoiding too many amorous individuals thinking that I was easy meat, I finally got next to the control room in a toilet. Perfect cover unless someone was too desperate to wait. Well, that's their problem. I had a big 'job' to do!

The over-sized phone I carried housed a neat little drill, which once I had located the cable, I carefully drilled into it, giving me room for the attachment. From the phone screen I could clone the presentation to look as if it was going according to plan. Then I waited for the big launch. My earpiece told me Olga was coaxing Dobrinsky and showering her with compliments. She can be so convincing!

The ball came to a halt ready for the finale, with the sponsors all waiting to congratulate themselves and Dobrinsky. As the main screen came into life, I waited for the moment to show the eager crowd where the funding had *really* come from for the venture. Instead of her grand presentation I fed the videos of her drug and sex dealings, with a few other juicy private bits the agency had supplied us with.

The gasps of shock and horror were echoing through the main hall, all the way to my private cubicle. Olga had the perfect viewpoint, telling me how Dobrinsky's smug expression morphed into the evil woman she hid. It sent her into a frenzy, shouting at her staff and criminal entourage to shut it down. Thing was, I was enjoying the show, and even though the damage was done, I left it running a bit too long. They put a search on the source, and they found me in the loo; so, I must give them the credit for that. Except it compromised my position forcing Olga to act beyond her remit.

Hearing my anxious gasps from tackling some muscley men, she went in for the kill. I was using JKD or Jeet Kune Do - something I studied from that great fighter Bruce Lee. Many useful late nights were spent in hotel rooms watching how he used speed and accuracy for disabling attackers.

However, on this occasion there were too many attackers and being only small, I was struggling. So, Olga took Dobrinsky, with a gun pinned to her back, into a separate room and forced her to withdraw her thugs from the restroom.

I managed to sidestep the others, dragging a ripped dress and ran for the landing stage where we had a boat waiting to escape. I watched through my enhanced glasses from the boat as Olga placed the gun at Dobrinsky's head and the resulting crack and exiting blood spray. I cringed because I knew she had gone too far - the agency would not be pleased with that. Olga then ended up in a gun battle with some other cronies but thankfully forced her way to meet me and we sped away across Lake Geneva.

***

My thoughts wander back into the bedroom and the dress that hugs perfectly around my body; the V-neck where the sapphire exquisitely rests in my cleavage. I suddenly get a feeling of warmth in my chest and admire my own shapely figure. This is unusual. I am not normally so aware of my own body, but this opportunity to dress up unlocks a femininity in me.

I gaze longingly into the mirror thinking of all the dances and parties I have missed over the years. Now death is following us around, maybe I need to find friends and have some fun for a change. A sadness sinks my heart with an icy chill - what friends? I have none. This life has extracted me from any meaningful relationships. That's why I desperately wanted to meet up with Freddie in Paris. He is one of the only guys I've ever connected with.

Frederick was also an orphan but raised in France by a diplomat and his wife. Well educated and fun, we met briefly in the Louvre when I had some time to kill, while Olga was killing someone else. His cheeky grin and *'lover-ly'* accent sent shivers down my back. He had an unusual haircut with one side shaved and the other swept over making him look like Marilyn Manson, without the manic crazy eyes.

We wandered around the halls not really taking much notice of the paintings and sculptures as we chatted and laughed. We sat outside by the pyramid eating McDonalds and ran through the fountains. It was a great day.

I try to resist a tear rolling down my cheek. It's times like this, when I stop and think too much, that sadness wells up. It's difficult to keep a lid on it. This house though seems to be breaking down my barriers. Maybe Anton, who seems to know me, has eroded my self-preservation - my protective barrier.

As I shift and sway, the necklace reflects the moonlight, and it nearly blinds me leaving a flash on my retina. Rubbing my eye, I notice something weird in the mirror. Moving closer I can see a pattern, like a laser print. Is that writing? I withdraw as I notice the sapphire is glowing and emitting more than a reflection. It's projecting something. Peering like an old woman, I begin to read:

"This protocol is for Marian Greene. Submit the encrypted password and await instructions."

Who is Marian Greene?

10 - The Church

The morning sun washes my face with a summery warmth, as I stretch out on silken sheets. I must have fallen into a deep sleep as the plum dress is still wrapped around me. I fight the tangled fabric and swing my legs across the edge of the bed. Yawning, I crack my neck and smell my own bad breath from last night's curry. Yuck! Where's the mouthwash?

The bathroom is a palace for my weary body, and I crash into the bath filling nicely with bubbles. I hear Olga banging around downstairs giving me hope that she had a reasonable night's sleep too.

"Hey, Olga! How are you doing this morning?" I shout, my voice like an old smoker.

"Good, my love; just making some breakfast. You?"

"Better for that sleep. What's the plan for today?" I really couldn't care less to be honest. I would rather just chill and explore the area.

"I need to contact the agency and find out who is behind this attack on us. I'm not taking any more crap from these people."

My sentiments precisely.

I slip into the silky warmth and submerge myself for as long as I can. Holding my breath has always been a problem. As a seven-year-old Olga took me swimming in a river where the current swept me away. I must have been underwater for minutes, panic racing through my chest. I couldn't breathe. The pain of water flooding my lungs was excruciating. A vigilant grandfather who was fishing, managed to rescue me and pumped my chest to get the water out. I was terrified. So, whenever I can, I force myself to meet the fear of drowning, even if it's in the bath.

Holding my nose, the air bubbles through my mouth until I can't stay under anymore. I surface like some whale, mouth wide open gasping for air. I'm not sure if this is working or not. My heart feels like it's exiting my mouth. If we were meant to be like fish … you know.

The whistling of a kettle and the aroma of croissants and coffee drift up the stairs. I wrap the white bathrobe snugly around my damp body which comforts me like a long-lost friend. There's a lightness to my steps this morning as I amble to the kitchen. To see Olga fully dressed, looking ready for an executive meeting, makes me wonder what she's up to.

"Wow, you're smart. Off to see someone?" I say winking.

"I feel more empowered if I'm appropriately dressed for any contact with the agency. They are our employer and I have always maintained professionalism with them." Of course, you have. I have known you talk to them in nothing more than your knickers and bra. Why is this different I wonder?

"I'm going to meet up with one of the executive members, so I am wanting to show that we must get to the bottom of this quickly. You'll have to amuse yourself today, Maisie."

"Ok, sounds good to me. Are you sure it's safe? I mean, we have been attacked three times in the last day. What if they are behind it? Should I be with you for extra cover?" I am wondering why this meeting seems less risky.

"No... it's fine Maisie - you are safer here. Make sure that you …"

"... keep a low profile - for God's sake *I know*!"

"Good."

"I met Anton last night by the way…" I say and see Olga's nervous twitch crank up.

"Who the hell is Anton?"

"The computer."

"The computer? *What computer?*"

"The one that knows who I am, apparently."

"Knows what? *Who*?" Her hand reaches for her gun holster, which is empty. Shit! Does she not know about Anton? My mind is trying to connect the dots here.

"You don't know about the computer? I thought with the biometrics that you knew the house is run by Anton, like an advanced Alexa." She shakes her head, her eyes flashing around the room.

"Where is it, Maisie? It might be a trick."

"*You* said this was a safe house, so I didn't think it was trying to kill us. He's a bit annoying to be honest, but not part of our funeral. Why are you so freaked out? He does as he's told - mainly."

Olga gives me that weird look - one of concern and crazy unpredictability. Is she going to find it and rip it out? I notice the red light on the camera flickering on. Pointing up to it, I retell my first encounters with it. She purses her lips as if she's holding her composure. Asking me to replay the episode to get the desktop to flip comes to nothing. Perhaps I need to get more blood. I ask Anton to come to life but no reply. Maybe I hurt its non-existent feelings. Anyway, Olga gives up and leaves me to eat breakfast alone.

I find some of my clothes that aren't bullet ridden and wave goodbye to Anton who has yet to resurface.

Carrying a banana and a drink, I venture outside. The house is set in large grounds overlooking farmland with a mixture of apple trees and meadow grass. Butterflies drift around in billowing warm air. My mind is so calm - a million miles from our manic assassin world. I find a swing hung from a large oak tree and sit pondering over last night's encounter with the necklace and Anton.

How come Olga has this as a safe house but doesn't know about Anton? Has he been installed recently? But he knows about the previous owners. And all that tech? What's behind the bookcase?

I am thinking too much again, and conspiracy theories invade my peace. I jump off and kick the loose grass and spot another building on a nearby hill. Looks like a church.

I've always been fascinated by these buildings. All over Europe they represent times when people needed God to watch over them. It seems to me not many need it that much these days. But maybe that's a false impression. I know at times I have prayed when a job is going wrong or we are in a tight position, and I don't lie when I say this, but I have felt someone help us through. Things happen when I pray, things I can't explain.

The hill is short and steep, and the small graveyard is neatly kept and well-trimmed. From here I can see the house and admire its position in the valley. Swallows swoop over the mowed grass, gobbling up flies and bugs flying around the church's weathered stone. I notice a couple of gravestones that look fresher than some of the others. Brushing off the dried grass cuttings I step back, realising whose grave this is.

Here lies in sweet peace until her heavenly Lord returns.

Her voice now joins the angels.

Maria Giogorgi

Dearly loved and missed by her family.

"This is the woman in the pictures," I say out loud. "So, she is dead. But why would she have all that tech? An opera singer doesn't normally give you the impression they need a super-duper Alexa - or Anton!" I switch my attention to the stone standing next to it. This one appears to be her husband, James. I scan the dates on both.

Died 5 September 2010

"Wow, they both died on the same day. That's tragic."

"It was my dear."

I swing around falling over the flower stand in front of the graves. A chill runs down my back; I didn't hear anyone approaching. I am so on point with people creeping up on me usually.

"Shit... you scared the life out of me!" I look up into an old lady's crinkly smiling face. "Sorry - I shouldn't have sworn." She kept on smiling and nodded. Leaning on her walking stick, she offers a hand. I thought I would pull her over, but her grip is strong and sturdy. "Thanks."

"They were a beautiful couple. She had the most exquisite voice. Such a waste when they passed away," the old lady says and smiles as a tear criss-crossed down her lined cheek.

"You knew them well then?" I ask, intrigued.

"Yes, you could say that... I was her mother." Wow, I feel heat racing up my neck for being an idiot gawping at her daughter's grave.

"How did they die on the same day? Was it a crash or something?" I ask, now wishing I had more tact.

"It was an accident from what I have been told. They were on a trip abroad and something happened on a boat. They lost my granddaughter too, but she has no grave here as they couldn't find her body. Only my memories survive now."

Her face reflected the loss still as fresh as the day it happened. I smile sympathetically and place a hand on her thin freckled skin.

"Gosh, I am so sorry. Was that their place?" I point down to Blue Haven. The old lady nods.

"Yes, not many people come and visit these days. It doesn't belong to the family anymore, as we had to sell. Some foreign person bought it, I think." She shakes her head. "I look down at the cottage every day and wish I had one last day with them. Especially my granddaughter - she was so full of beans." I see a twinkle in her eye. "So mischievous and such a loving child. She would run rings around us all." She gazes at me with her bright blue eyes. "Strange to see someone looking at their graves. Do you live around here? I've not seen you before."

"No, I'm just visiting. But I am staying in the cottage. So, it's great to meet someone who knows about it and the people who owned it." She staggers back and gives me a harder stare. I hope that's not going to cause a problem. For a moment I feel her eyes are scanning me to extract some information. Then her eyes drift and she settles back on her stick.

"Are you the foreign lady who owns it?" she asks carefully.

"Oh no, my mom is probably the owner," I reply. "I didn't even know she had this place 'til yesterday. It was a great surprise when we arrived. So lovely, although some quirky things about it." At this comment, I wished my mouth would close, as I have already said too much.

Olga will be putting a contract out on the old lady just in case she's one of the death squad. She nods and smiles again.

"Do you know that her real name was Marian Greene?" she asks me, her brow furrowing.

My mind starts to connect the dots.

"It is strange that you should come now …" she drifts off again. What is strange?

"Oh, why?"

"It would have been my granddaughter's birthday today. I come here to say a prayer for her, that God would watch over her and keep her safe. Maybe she is still alive somewhere and He will bring her back home one day." Her eyes fill up again. My eyes fill up too, thinking what an amazing lady to keep that sort of vigil all these years.

"I say prayers sometimes … usually to get us out of trouble!" I am not sure if being light-hearted is the best response, but it makes her giggle. She reaches out a hand and squeezes mine.

"You have great faith young lady, never stop praying!" Well, I don't think I agree, but maybe I should pray more and smile back.

"Well, my dear, have a lovely stay and I hope you find everything you are looking for."

With that, she hobbles off back towards the church. I shout my thanks and tell her to take care. I still feel the impression of her hand on mine, a warmth and care that is foreign to me. I stay a while and take in the view looking across meandering stones walls and sheep grazing. My thoughts engage with the old lady's wishes that she would indeed see her family again.

11 - The Secret

It was nice to meet that old lady today; it gives me a sense of grounding in something more than the uncertain world I have always known. Wandering down the hill, the sun warms my body and my heart. I'm sensing my hard-nosed attitude towards life is melting, allowing other feelings I have suppressed to poke their heads through holes in my emotions.

It must have been a lovely family to be a part of, to live here and travel the world appearing at concerts, having the adulation of people. That's something we have never had; just a payoff, a contract complete and move on to the next. No feelings of appreciation or a job well done. Well, that's me… I am sure that Olga *does* get a sense of satisfaction about her work. To me, it's a bit ghoulish, this 'dispatching' of people. She seems to enjoy the whole process. From the first message to the escape from the scene; it gives her a thrill which I rarely share.

Entering through the blue garden gate, the car is still missing so Olga must be having a good long chat about life and death. The biometric key works for me and the front door clicks open. Shutting it casually behind me, I glance up and see the red-light flicker. Anton is awake.

"Ok Anton, what's up with you today? Why didn't you show when Olga wanted to see you?"

"As I have said before, I am programmed to make sure you are safe. Olga Gabrys poses a threat to your wellbeing." I cross my arms and skew my lips.

"Ok, but *why*? What threat is she? Surely the biggest threat are these people who are trying to kill us. Do you know about those then, bigshot?"

"Of course, it would be a mistake for me not to know there are contracts out on you both." I throw out my hands in horror. He *does* know about them.

"Olga has gone to find out what's going on. So, instead we could have just asked you... you *moron*."

"Well... yes. But that is not the point. My primary objective is to get you to safety. Olga has been reckless over the years with you beside her and now certain organisations are wanting to terminate her - and you, unfortunately." I shake my head.

"So... how much danger *are* we in Anton? What else are you not telling me?" This guy is getting to be a pain in the arse.

"I must advise you that certain things will be a shock and perhaps an unwanted revelation about your situation. Maybe you want to ask me some questions to get us started. If you go to the library, I can best show you." I hurriedly walk through the kitchen and grab a jar of cookies and a coke before settling down on the squeaky chair.

"Do I stab myself to make you pop up again?"

"No, you are accepted as the authentic administrator of the house and its contents. Please sit and I will start." Oh, I do feel important…

The screen flips effortlessly before me, and the bookcases split open and disappears into the walls. Well, that confirms I wasn't dreaming!

"So, my first question is… why all this high-tech stuff in a soprano's home?" My question is muffled as I munch on a cookie.

"It started back in 1999 when the relations between certain countries were teetering on the brink of war. MI6 was involved in many overseas operations to create stable governments to prevent a meltdown by various states which would lead to worldwide wars which no one state could influence or control any longer. The code name for this operation was 'TROJAN'."

My heart jumps.

"Operatives were sent undercover to these states to ascertain who could be trusted with the technology and arms to prevent these destabilising factions from succeeding. Marian Greene and her husband James were key operatives in this."

"I know about this from a dossier that Olga gave me - but it said these were people sent by MI6 to *destabilize* these nations, not help them. So, it's the direct opposite of what you have said. There is so much fake news around, I'm not sure what to believe anymore."

"All about the perspective - who is telling the story; the freedom fighter being the hero or the villain. What I have explained is the true reason behind the operations. Marian was a well-known opera singer giving her valid reasons and cover for meeting up with their counterparts.

Her and James were about to uncover secrets about an organisation which would benefit more than any other from a destabilized world. My data banks hold the list of all the dark operatives that this organization has in action. It is safe here and cannot be hacked into. James ensured that I was secure from any prying eyes. That is why I think they were killed."

"Killed? It wasn't an accident then? I met a lady at the church who said she was Marian's mother and she said it was an accident on a boat."

"Yes… as you have said, fake news is everywhere misdirecting people. I shall show you clips from their work."

The blinds on the windows fall and shut out the sunlight as the glow from the screen fills the room. I watch as the couple I saw before now are seen meeting with different key army personnel and businesspeople. Tech drawings and lists of equipment and arms rolled up the screen, along with lists from various factions considered either volatile or cooperative.

It's all a bit mesmerizing and I keep blinking to concentrate. Anton is on overdrive now, divulging all his well-hidden secrets. I try to stop the flow of information for a second.

"Hold on a minute - the next question is, why have you shown me all this and not Olga? She would surely know who would be best to take this information to. Even sell it for a massive price," I ask puzzled.

"This is not for sale Maisie. It's your insurance policy."

"*Eh?*"

"It is meant for your eyes only - then to carry on the work," he states. I stare blankly at the screen, feeling a weird sensation rising through my belly and back.

What does he mean; *insurance policy ... carry on the work*...I am not happy about what he is saying. I can't understand why this is all for me and not Olga. Clearly, Anton does not trust her. Next question.

"Why don't you trust Olga? She has looked after me ever since I was an orphan. She has protected me through thick and thin. I cannot see why she is to be kept out of the loop."

"This is difficult, but I must show you Maisie…" The screen rolls on and a list of 'dark operatives' appear in alphabetical order. It stops at the Gs', and I read a name which I don't want to, along with a picture.

"Dark Operative - Section C - Lithuanian assassin - OLGA ALEXANDRIA GABRYS."

"What? She's a … '*dark operative*'? I have never seen her doing anything remotely dark! This doesn't tie up with what I know of her. We live in each other's pockets, day after day. There's no way she is one of these - *things*! This has to be wrong," I spurt out, staring wildly at the screen and shaking my head.

"It is *true* Maisie. I have footage of her dealings with other dark operatives." On screen, I watch videos of other meetings, names and pictures extracted from his list confirming their allegiance to this underworld. These are locations I remember well.

She always told me she was seeing her love interests. *Really*? This is what she was *doing*? My emotions are fighting with it all; sweat and anger mixed with betrayal. The images of other dark operatives flashed up along with the confirming details and pictures at all the locations we had been over the years; so many, it's doing my head in.

My mind is all over the place, a fuzzy mess; I can't think straight. Tears flood my eyes. I have never felt so annoyed. My heart is racing to get out of my chest. She has held so much from me, all these years. How could she? *Bastard*! NO, *worse*. I push the chair back and shout as loud as I can.

"*BASTAAAAARD*!!"

I fling the coke bottle as hard as I can, smashing it into the opposite wall. I don't know what to do. My life has suddenly been ripped from underneath my feet. The one I have trusted and tolerated all these years is a charlatan, a fake. I want to smash her head in. But no… I must get the truth from her. Am I just to accept this version of history from a computer that I've only known for a couple of days? No… I must get Olga to be real with me, give her a chance to tell the truth and deny this whole fiasco.

Man, I am so mixed up. It feels like my hormones have exploded all at once. I am full of rage and yet I'm gaping down a hole of despair opening around me. The words of the old lady flash through my mind "…*never stop praying…*" perhaps this is one of those times.

Prayer better save Olga from my hands if this turns out to be true.

12 - The Other Stranger

It seems that my whole life has been a fantasy, a starring role in a film I was totally unaware of. I'm keeping away from any potential weapons as I might regret what I'll do if I lose it. Anton continued to tell me more about the clandestine agency which refers all the work to us and how it is seen as one of those which would benefit from a chaotic world.

Even though I thought we were doing the world a service by getting rid of all these scumbags, it seems there were other reasons behind it. Each one we dispatched made way for the people the *agency* wanted to replace them with. These were then left in peace to operate without any interference. What a con! I have been a part of a worldwide con job, facilitating organised crime syndicates to thrive. I feel ashamed and used. *Arrrrgh*!! I'm so angry! She is going to get such a mouth full!

Anton decided to keep the contents of the bookcase hidden for the time being as he wanted to see what happens after my confrontation with Olga. He said he wanted to keep out of it. Typical bloke! Keep your head down while all the crap is flying and then come up smelling of roses! Well, not quite… he's the one that has created this shit storm, so he better back up all that he started.

I'm sweating like a geyser, and my fingers are hurting as I've been banging the walls in frustration. What's taking so long? Is she seeing more dark, sodding operatives? I yank open the fridge and grab some cheese and pizza and another coke.

Striding outside the fresh air gives me some relief. The house was becoming stifling and pushing in on me. I must get control of myself, so I don't look like a lunatic and make nonsense of what I'm accusing her of. Otherwise, she will tell me to get to my room and lock the door until I settle down. This is not something that can be swept under the carpet. I have got to go head-to-head with her. I run through my script over and over trying to make it coherent and not a load of drivel. Why can't Anton just explain, he knows more than me? Even computers are chicken!

My heart flutters as I hear a crunching of gravel and the quiet rolling of a car pulling up to the house. It must be Olga. I run and then pace myself to meet her at the front door. Breathing deeply, I try to calm my nerves. It's not working. I am scratching my jeans and biting my lip till it hurts. All the training in martial arts isn't helping either. It usually enables me to manage my nerves, but this is personal, different to all the anonymous 'dispatches'. Getting this right matters more than anything. I stand before the door rocking on my feet, flexing my muscles. *Come on, open the damn door!*

I hear the click and immediately tense up. Blowing my cheeks, I brace myself for the explosion that is about to come. I feel a breeze move my hair around, sweeping it across my face. I swish it back in irritation. I need to look into her eyes; they will tell me straight away if she is lying. Then doubt fills my mind. *What if it's true?* Then all my life has been a lie and I can't guarantee that I *will* know if she is lying to me. What the hell! Here we go.

Olga walks in - but not alone. *Who the hell is this?* I back away from this mystery man. What is she doing bringing someone here? A safe house is supposed to be - *safe*! My instincts are telling me to be wary and I slip into defence mode, taking a non-threatening stance but ready for action. Olga looks directly at me, trying to draw my attention, but I'm focused on this intruder. He is broad and evidently athletic. Shaved head and dressed in casual summer gear, his shades sit on the end of his nose, his arms strong, fight ready. He has a Southeast Asian look about him.

"No need to get all stupid Maisie; this is Lee. He is here to help us out. Lower your guard. I know it's a surprise that I've brought someone here, but it's for a good reason." Yeah, to beat the crap out of me!

"And what *help* is *he* going to give, *Olga*?" She flinches at my terse reply and the slightest flicker runs across her eyebrow. I'm not making this easy for her. She is fully aware of what I am capable of, and 'Lee' will meet the full wrath of my anger if this turns nasty. His next move takes me by surprise. He launches himself and tries to bear hug me but I'm too quick and kick him where all men love to be kicked - *not*!

"Keep away from me you... you *bastard*!" He reels backwards and tries to regain some composure. The shades are not sitting so well on his nose and make him look foolish. I glance at Olga. *She is pulling a gun on me!* I dive through the nearest doorway, hoping I can get away through an outside exit. I feel a sharp pain in my leg. *Damn!* What just hit me?

I run towards the open door that leads out into the garden. But for some reason my leg isn't responding. It feels dead, full of pins and needles. *Needles!* I look down and see a dart stuck in my calf. She's darted me like a bloody wild animal! My head feels fuzzy, and I can't see straight... I'm grasping the door handle to steady me.

... all I see is a blurry vision of colours and shifting objects.

....my hands reach out to catch my free fall.

... I'm sure I just hit the flagstones, but I feel nothing.

... I'm

... not here...

where ammm I ...?

13 - The Rescue

Is that splashing water? ... My body shivers... my eyes are stapled together... Why can't I see anything? Then I realise what's wrong. My eyes *are* open but staring at darkness. I grasp at the void and hold onto nothing. Fear pushes up through my throat like a serpent escaping its lair. *Where am I?*

I grope around and bash my fingers on cold slimy stuff, hard and uncompromising. *What's this?* I slip into deeper water and the cold bites as life comes back to my legs. Water is all around me, at about waste height, freezing and spiking my fragile state. *Where has she put me?* My foot slips on the slimy ground. *Crack*! That's my head by the way... ouch - *bloody* ouch! Somehow, it wakes me up even more.

Now I'm searching for some spec of light to get my bearings. Looking up I see a small bright eye looking back at me. Then I see it's not an eye, but daylight. I shake my head and rub my eyes trying to focus. It looks like the end of a long tunnel with a light inviting me to come out. But I can't. Whatever I touch is slimy and the prison is wider than I can reach across. Shit! Am I in a well? *Olga has put me in a well!!*

The platform I was originally perched on is just above the water level, so I try to clamber onto it again, flinching as my fingers scrape against the rocks. Damn.

My nails will never recover from this. *Why am I thinking about my nails?* Perched again I can't believe Olga had drugged me and thrown me down a well. Great! That has to confirm everything that Anton has told me. *She is a dark operative.* Why has she put me here though and not dispatched me like the rest? Oh man, I don't care. I'm alive – for now. I must work on how to get out of this. An unwelcome noise distracts my thinking. A whoosh of cold air hits my shivering body, followed by a gurgling sound. Oh god, that's not more water, please?

It gushes in from the darkness, an unstoppable force splashing my face, chilling me even more. *I must get out of here.* My muscles tense up and my throat tightens. I have that uncontrollable feeling of doom creeping over my common sense. I clam up and can't move. What if the water gets too deep? Can I swim upwards, or will I sink like a stone? My only response is to go into a trance.

"Come on Maisie - this is not the time to die! I'm going to die? Thanks for that! I was wondering..." This pep talk isn't going well. "No time for puns, just look around - there has to be steps or something." Groping again I find nothing that will support my feet. The water keeps on rising. Now lapping over my legs, I don't want to fall, it will be so much deeper. Biting my lip, I really don't know what to do. Tears fill my eyes. I can't believe that Olga would do this to me after all this time. She has been

my mother, teacher, and protector since I can remember. *What has changed?*

Two days ago, we were in a classy French boutique restaurant and then all hell broke loose. Is she really killing me? I shake the water off my head. It's splashing higher and higher. My hair sticks to my face. *Oh my god, I'm going to drown.* I can't shake off this fear. It's closing in on me faster than the dark freezing water. My mind flips to all the amazing places we have been, the warm sunny locations, the glamorous shopping sprees on the streets of Milan and Rome. Has it come to this? It makes no sense. The water is now gripping my waste and the cold is dulling my mind. I must shout for help. Perhaps someone will hear.

"Help...*HELP!!*" My voice is squeaky and shrill. This will never get anyone's attention. *Keep trying you idiot.*

"HELP... I'M DOWN THE WELL... HELP!!!" Desperation is choking me. I'm crying uncontrollably. My fears are recreating my despair in the river. Who's going to rescue me this time?

"HELP... HELP... *HELP*!!" My neck is now barely keeping my chin out of the water. The splashing is stinging my eyes and panic hurts my chest. I'm on my tip toes trying to take breaths as this watery grave is dragging me into its evil clutches. I can't shout anymore. My last thoughts are a jumble as my head is submerged.

"Please help me someone... I don't want to die. If you are there, God... please help me..." My mind begins to drift and the pain of trying to keep air in my lungs rips at my chest. This is it... my last breath... it's gone. I must not breathe in water...

I hear a voice... Who is that? Is it God answering? He sounds familiar... posh and straight forward. Unemotional and practical... not how I expected God to be. I can't hold on anymore and I breathe in...

Warmer air envelops my dying breath, water filling my body. I hear that voice again. Everything I see is in a blur. Light is all around me as I feel transported away from my watery pit. Is this heaven or something? My mind drifts in and out of reality. I'm floating. A blanket of warmth covers my body, and my fears melt away... I give in.

Blackness.

***

Light, so bright, pushes its way through my eyelids, painful but welcoming and I feel my body enclosed in soft warmth. I dare to open my eyes, squinting. My body shivers as I find myself, not in heaven, but in a bed. Lifting my head, I just make out a wardrobe and flowery curtains.

"Where am I?" Thinking this was a private question, someone answers.

"Safe little one... safe." I look across to where the voice came from and as my eyes adjust. I see the smiling face of the old lady I met at the church. Blinking, I shake my head again. Water pours out of my ears.

"How...How did you get me here?"

"It seems that my suspicious nature got the better of me as I had a phone call from someone called Anton asking me to go to the old family well because someone needed help."

I prop myself up with the soft pillows so I can look directly at her. Anton *rang* her? He knew I was in danger. What he said about keeping me safe... it's his directive. It's what he has been doing since I've been here. Was that the posh voice I heard?

"He rang *you*? How did he know I was down there?"

"He only said he had heard you shouting, and I needed to get help and drag you out. I got my grandson to help me. We managed to lift you out with a pulley and got a paramedic to check you over. It was a good job we found you in time, as you could have drowned." My hands are shaking as I thank her. The weight of my head forces it to sink back into the welcoming pillows.

"I'm glad you are ok. You need to rest though. Have a sleep and I will bring you something warm and filling to give you a boost." She smiles and walks off holding onto her stick. The click of the door triggers the sleep my body needs and again I drift off into contented darkness.

***

I stir, at what time I'm not sure. I glance at my watch; 22.30. I must have been here all day. Darkness fills the window and moonlight glances off the bed cover. It's reassuringly warm and cosy. Snuggling down into the duvet, I try to get my thoughts into some sort of order. I feel so weak, but anger and hurt are building like a thunderstorm. Yet, gratitude and relief briefly push it aside, thankful that I have an Anton and old lady looking after me. That was so close. I could have died. Maybe someone *is* watching over me after all.

I spy my clothes neatly folded on a chair as I run my fingers over what I'm dressed in. A cotton nightdress, one which would not look out of place in a Jane Austen movie. I stagger across to the loo and sit pondering over what has happened.

Did Olga really try to kill me? I wonder where she is now. And Lee; I knew he looked shifty. I hope I sent his love expectations back a few years! Anger is driving me to get back to the house and see if they are still there, but I feel like the blood is draining from my body down the loo. Maybe I need to recover a bit first.

"If Olga is against me, along with the agency, who do I turn to?" My breathing speeds up. I shake my head, realising that I am all but alone. "There is Anton, but he's a bloody computer. I need people who I can rely upon. *Who, though?*" My mind is in a whirl again, and I wish I'd stayed in the safe warm bed. I hear a click at the door and tense up. I hear the stick of the old lady clunking on the wooden floor.

"Hello my dear. I've brought you some hot chocolate. Hope you are feeling better."

"Yes, thanks. Just a bit confused, but I had a good sleep. Hmm, tell me something… when you got to the well, did you see anyone else around? A car parked at the gate or anything?"

I hear a chink of the cup being placed on a table. Then a muffled shuffle of feet in loose fitting slippers.

"Not that I remember dear. It was quiet and peaceful. It has been a long time since I went down to the well. Nearly forgot where it was. My grandson found it though and used the old pulley for the water to pull you up and out. He is such a clever boy." And I am incredibly grateful for his help.

"What's his name? I would like to thank him sometime." I hear another shuffle as she is leaving.

"Archie, he lives in the village. I'm sure he would love to see you too." The door clicks shut, and I smell the chocolate drifting around the room. I am overwhelmed by her care and tears fill my eyes. I feel really loved for once and not just used. Taking the hot chocolate, it's having a calming effect on my jangled nerves. As I slurp the steaming drink, I can't stop thinking what I'm going to do with Olga.

14 - The Safe

I decided to sleep over at the old lady's house as I felt so weak and rubbish. Glad I did. The smell of lush bacon wafts up the stairs. Getting showered and dressed quickly, I stumble down the wooden staircase and meet the old lady sitting by an open fire with a cat on her lap.

"Oh, good morning little one. I hope you slept well. I've taken the liberty and made you a fried breakfast. I hope that is, ok?" She smiles, knowing full well I'm happy with that, as I'm drooling.

"Thank you so much. I can't say how grateful I am - you saved my life."

What I said shocks me, but there it is. I was so nearly a goner. Dispatched by my own mother and … dickhead Lee! I sit by the fire and tuck into the plate of egg, bacon, beans, and potato wedges. I'm stuffing my face as if I'm a homeless kid. Then I briefly stop and consider… that is what I am… The old lady rattles the fire with her poker and distracts me.

"I had a quiet look around Blue Haven and I couldn't see anyone there this morning, so I think that whoever was there has left." She smiles and shows the outline of her dentures. A shiver runs down my back, considering how dangerous that could have been, with Olga and Lee knocking around. Maybe it will be safe to go back. I need to get my stuff … and talk to Anton who needs some thanks too, I guess. I slurp a huge cup of tea she has poured for me and explain I must get back to the house.

"You didn't get the police involved yesterday, did you?" I don't want them to start snooping around. That would make life far too complicated.

"No dear, just a paramedic friend who checked you over. He lives in the village too, so was quick to come up and make sure you were alright. I was going to send you to hospital, but he reassured me you would be ok." Smiling, she strokes the cat like a Bond villain.

"So many people to thank. What a great place to live with all these kind folk around. I must see them sometime. But first I must get back to the house. I've got a few things to sort out."

After petting the cat and hugging the old lady, I scramble up the hill towards Blue Haven. Fighting back the tears, I open the gate and stand a minute scared over what I'm going to find. It all appears to be locked up and secure. Could Olga have changed the security so no one can get in? Only one way to find out. I press the biometric key thing. My eyes open wide, half expecting a swinging blade to slice off my head. The door clicks open. Phew! No traps … yet.

I glance around the hallway, checking to see whether any trip wires or other boobytraps have been set. My training never leaves me, I'm primed for every eventuality, or so I thought. The red LED flashes on Anton's eye. At least he's still working.

"Hey, Anton. What's happened here?"

I can see that the rooms are not as neat and tidy as they were, with papers and paintings scattered in random piles. I make my way to the library. I stumble for a second as I'm shocked by what I see. The whole room has been smashed and ripped apart. The desk where Anton usually talks to me has been shredded. The bookcase lies in ruins, with all the books tossed in heaps. I get the impression that Olga was trying to find Anton, and whatever is behind the bookcase.

"Anton, are you still with me? This is a bloody mess!"

The light on the camera flickers on. I hear a weird sound, like a crow and cat together trying to speak. I search through the piles of torn paper and find the source of the noise. Looks like a speaker. Anton's voice painfully grates through it.

"Oh my god. Are you ok?" I hold the speaker closer, trying to hear what he's saying.

"Open the bookcase please…" I just about make out. How do I do that, with no biometric fingerprint jobo? I strain to hear again. "Say the words 'Maisie. Protocol 469 Echo Charley Victor'"

Oh, ok. It's that easy. I say the password and the remnants of the bookcase begin to creak and groan. I can see books and bits of wood getting caught in the movement, and so I chuck stuff out of the way. There… that should make it easier.

The steel door stands in all its glory, defying all who enter. I peer at the thick handle and the mechanism that sits on the front. I wonder; how do I get into this? Anton's muffled voice directs me again.

"Press the handle to the right with your left hand and grasp firmly as you place your eye to the retinal scanner above it."

I raise my eyebrows and obey. I'm getting a tingle of excitement as to what I'm going to find in this fortress. It looks as if, despite Olga and Lee's best efforts, they could not get anywhere near it. Anton has done good. The whirring of gears and clanking vibrate the steel structure and I step back thinking it's going to open. Then, the noise stops. Nothing happens. What? Doesn't it recognise me?

"Anton… What's going on? It's not opening. Should I have done something else?"

His silence worries me. Has he lost power? Have they damaged him? A few seconds later I'm pacing up and down thinking that whatever is hidden is going to remain that way. There must be a different route. Maybe he needs to reboot or something. Then I remember some kit I have with me that might help. I run upstairs to where I left my bags.

I hope Olga hasn't taken my phone and stuff. My heart jumps with anger as I see all my clothes and personal stuff are scattered mercilessly all over the room. Torn and shredded are my treasured crop tops and jeans. All my work equipment has been trashed. I stand and stare wanting to smash something. Then, I search frantically for my phone. It's the one thing I need now to bring me hope. I feel around the base of the bed. Instinct has taught me to hide what is most dear and lifesaving to me, even if we were in a safe house, and supposedly ok with Mumsie! I grope around praying that it is still there. My fingers touch the familiar tacky surface of the cover. Yes!

Out from its hiding place, I swipe the screen. All seems ok. My finger hovers over the screen as I hesitate; maybe using it would send an alert to Olga, so I power down. Then I remember Frederick, my on-the-hold boyfriend, showed me a useful hack to stop anyone tracking my phone. I hold the power and camera button together and speak, 'Encryption code 25795 - Maisie'. He assured me that would work. I never tried it as I thought he was off his trolley. How would he know how to stop a tracker? Now should not be the time to try out his theory, but I'm desperate.

As I clamber back down the stairs, I say the code again and wait. The phone screen flashes into life and a new picture comes up. I grimace as it's *not* what I expected. A picture of Freddie appears laughing. Oh no, the idiot has sent me a stupid hack to give me his profile picture. What a prat! I feel heat on my face and swear words pour into my head. This idiot has now ruined my phone. I ram it into my pocket and scream as I am now without any form of communication or power. I kick the nearest thing and resist despair forcing me to cry.

Hearing a buzzing sound, I yank the phone out and see that an incoming call is flashing on the screen. It's a number I don't recognise. Who is it? Is it a trap from Olga or Lee, or the agency; or worse still those who have a contract out on me? Doubt fills my mind. Do I answer? Oh, sod it. I press the screen. I wait for a voice, or noise. Nothing. Not even a whisper of breath. Then I hear it. Some sort of electronic sound. Anton suddenly speaks again, muffled.

"Hold the phone near the door…" he says. Ok, so what now? I hold it close to the steel door. The electronic sound grows louder, and a reply comes from the door. They are talking to each other! Clicks and clunking echoes in the room as the door moves and the handles start to whizz around. This giant safe door opens effortlessly. I pull back and stare in amazement.

Stepping through the opening, I gaze at the vastness of this hidden room. It opens out wider than the library behind me and is divided into other rooms further along. It must extend into the rock outcrop behind the house. The first one has books along with files and surveillance equipment. There are other cabinets that are sealed to the left and right. The next room opens out showing racks of weapons and equipment. Wow! This is an assassin's Aladdin's cave! The walls are dripping with everything from assault rifles to stun grenades, handguns, and tasers. I have never seen such an array of weapons. The agency would dearly like to have their hands on this. I can see why Olga and Lee had a go at breaking in. Anton speaks up now, clearer, and more urgently.

"As you see I wanted to protect this array of weapons and more importantly, the information my data holds. Their attempts at breaking in were futile, as James ensured that no one was able to breach the security. Now Maisie - I hope you have recovered after the experience down the well?"

"Yes - thanks to you I am. Did you phone the old lady?"

"Indeed - I thought it best to get you out before you drowned."

"Er... *yes* that was the right decision!" I can't believe he is so clinical about it all.

"If you don't mind me saying, I did warn you how dangerous Olga is to you."

"Yes... you did... and I'm incredibly grateful that you rescued me. But why did she want to kill me? And who was this bloke, Lee?" A screen flashes up alongside me, with the details and pictures of the man called 'Lee'. I read about this dark operative who works with the agency and watch as videos play of Olga and him on operations. I shake my head. Anger rises like the incoming tide. Everything is a lie.

"It is imperative that we work together and stop the agency from continuing to undo 'TROJAN'. We will run through all the contacts you need to make and others who can help you." Shaking my head, I take a long look around this cave of death. I can't believe what is happening to me. I am suddenly on a mission to stop my mother and the agency who has been our mainstay all these years. I am curious who these 'others' are.

"Anton – who are these other people you want me to hook up with?"

"Your only hope of stopping Olga and the agency."

"So, is Olga and the agency working together?"

"Now the truth has been revealed, they no longer see eye to eye. Olga is now outside the agency and therefore is being hunted by other organisations."

I'm both delighted that someone has her as a mark but also wary of the agency's intentions.

"So, what does the agency think of me?"

"A threat and an asset simultaneously."

Oh, that's reassuring.

"So, now that you are including me in this world of yours, you have effectively made me an even greater target than before!"

Thanks Anton… I really thought you cared.

"It was inevitable Maisie – you cannot escape your destiny." Now I am *Luke Skywalker*.

I jump up, the chair spiralling away. My mother was trying to kill me along with unknown assassins lurking everywhere. Why do I need this in my life?

"They will be aware of your heritage. The extent of your knowledge is unknown to them, but if Olga has said anything to them about me, then they will be anxious to acquire my data and dispose of you." Not so reassuring…and what is my *heritage*?

"I am unsure as to whether you have understood who you are?" he says mysteriously. "Or more to the point - who Marian and James were." Anton drops this as if it were a casual remark but leaves a shiver running down my back.

"What do you mean?"

"They were your British birth parents."

I feel like a truck has just smashed into my head.

***

I collapse on to a chair, choked up with conflicting thoughts. *They were my parents?* They were agents working for MI6, under surveillance by the agency. No wonder I have weird flashbacks of opera singers. Tears race down my cheeks. My head feels woozy as I gaze at the flagstone floor, biting my lip wondering what on earth I am going to say to Olga when I see her again.

This revelation is too much for me. I thought they abandoned me as a five-year-old child. Then it comes to me like an avalanche. The old lady is my *grandmother*! I fall to my knees, holding my head in sweaty hands. She has been praying to see me for all these years and I turn up… *on my birthday!* That is so crazy.

Why did Olga adopt me? Did she find me in an orphanage after my parents were killed? Why didn't she tell me about them before? I sit crossed legged sobbing, abandoned again. This is my home, the house I would have spent five years growing up in, yet I remember nothing. And why did Olga buy it? She must have known about my parents and this house. Did she buy it out of some sort of sentimentality?

Tears roll off my nose and form a pool of salty water in a groove on the flagstone. This betrayal and cover up has been overwhelming. My mind is spinning out of control, and I get up clearing my nose out onto the floor. I stare vacantly into the remaining mirror on the wall. Am I really who Anton says I am? Doubt clouds everything I hold real. My eyes are cloaked in mist, reflecting my heart set adrift on a foggy sea.

15 - The Truth

I escape the house and sit on a solitary chair whilst my heart is chilled with a cruel internal breeze. The events of the past few days have wrecked me. I don't know what to think, believe or hope for. Getting away from *Darth* Anton is my priority now. I am not listening anymore to *'this is your destiny'* crap. Trying to imagine a life out of the ruins of this chaos, is only coming up with dead ends – literally.

Head in my hands, tears roll down my face again and I quietly sob. I can't see a way ahead. What future do I have, except on the run? I have no regular support, only the money that Olga so *generously* put into an expense account for me. That's probably all gone with her and Lee. A wave of dread looms over me.

A bird whistles above in a tree distracting me for a second. "I guess you don't have to think about assassins and mothers that betray you. All you need is here. Simple and uncomplicated. I wish my life were." It continues its impulsive song in reply.

I gaze at the house and try to place myself here as a child. It doesn't bring anything to mind, and I certainly can't remember a computer running it. I strain to recreate ghostly figures of my real mum and dad wandering around the garden pushing me on the swing, but nothing comes. The music, as irritating as it is, twinges at some memory but nothing I can grasp. Olga has done a complete whitewash of my earlier life.

What if the old lady would be of any help? She is my grandmother, after all. Even that holds a terror, as if I'm wrong, it would bring so much disappointment and pain. She has been praying for me all these years. I bet she didn't know what her daughter and son-in-law were really up to. It might just finish her off when she realises that I'm an assassin's assistant. Too many complications; the past is better left buried. Then I think of the cousin I have, Archie. Would he be of any help? Shaking my head, I know I can't rely on any of these people as they have normal lives and deserve them. I alone must make whatever I can of this mess.

My phone buzzes again. Who is this? Hesitating, I see *'no caller ID'*. Hmm…this could be dangerous. I'm so exhausted, do I really care? Taking a deep breath, I flick the screen biting my lip. The voice is clear and easily recognisable. Anton! Does he ever give up?

"Oh Anton – *what do you want?*"

"I am aware you are in a transition period, and it will be difficult to process. I am a digital construct, so processing evolving input is commonplace. For you, it is mixed up with emotions and decision making, causing conflicts and…"

"For f… sake, shut up you cretin! I am sick and tired of this drivel. Leave me alone to work this out. I can't do this with your voice rattling in my head!"

"Yes. I want to direct you to that end. When you are ready, I have something to show you. Whilst waiting for you, more details have emerged about your past."

"Ok… ok give me a break. I've had so much shit thrown at me to last a lifetime. I'll have a look in a bit."

***

I wander around the kitchen, which is tempting me to gorge, but my stomach is refusing, and I keep gagging as my fingers wander idly through the cupboards. My appetite is wrecked along with my life - *screwed*. Even the coke which I drink by the gallon, has little attraction.

Perhaps this is where alcohol comes into its own. So many people seem to resort to it at times like this. I doubt that would take away the pain though. I have seen the results too often. Olga, for example, used gin and vodka to settle herself down and usually ended up in a useless mess. Her boyfriends were quite happy for her to be legless so they could do whatever they wanted. No thank you; I'm not leaning on that prop. I need my wits to be on point, especially now. I snatch a lettuce leaf and grind my teeth.

"So sorry mum and dad that they smashed up your house. I will get it right again – I promise." A compulsion takes over and I place pots and glasses and furniture back in some sort of order. This is mine, after all – *not* Olga's.

How did she get it anyway? Why would she keep this place knowing it was mum and dads? Perhaps Anton could answer. A slice of pizza beckons, so I devour it in one. Then another. My appetite is returning. Finally, a rise of good feelings is strengthening me. Maybe I can listen to Anton again.

I drag myself back to the safe room, dreading whatever else this computer might shove in my face. The lights flicker on as I cross through the doorway and a screen brightly shines. Anton, ready as ever.

"I am glad you are back. Let me show you what I found." I halt his enthusiasm as my emotions are tender and raw. I cannot cope with any more surprises. However, I am curious about the bank of screens on the opposite wall.

"Anton; what do these screens link into?"

"They are worldwide surveillance systems. CIA, FBI, MI6, GCHQ, FSB, MSS, Mossad all feed into here. Trojan has access to all the major security protocols. Therefore, it has been possible to monitor your progress over the years." Monitor my progress? He's been watching me for *years?* Talk about a nanny state. A question gnaws at me.

"So, if you have watched me all this time, why has no one told me about the agency and its dodgy operations? Why didn't you come to my rescue earlier? A lot of unnecessary violence and killing could have been avoided." Anton takes a pause.

"I am aware that your life has been perilous and painful, but your journey has prepared you for this time. Even though the analogy of a parent isn't compatible with my programming, it is the nearest way I can express the way I view it." Anton is now comparing himself to a family member. *What a bloody cheek!*

"You have the skills and tenacity to see this through, along with a purpose to avenge your parents. Although I do not share such emotions, I perceive the need for a wrong to be reversed. Maybe an incorrect course to be redirected." What? *Avenge my parents?* Who does he mean?

"Have you not worked it out Maisie… your original name was Maisie Greene." Yes of course I have worked that out. What he says next though sends pain ripping through my mind.

"It was *Olga* that killed your parents…"

***

I sit crumpled inside as this latest truth drags my emotions ever further down into a murky abyss. Anton confirms what I am not wanting to accept, although with everything that has happened, why does it shock me so much? I wished for once though he didn't lack emotional filters, desiring some comfort and someone to hug. All I can find is a cushion and my own company.

I stare vacantly as I replay videos in my head of what my parents must have suffered, what I lost - all because of this stupid agency - and *Olga*. My mind is full of hatred wanting to crush her in any way that will cause her pain - the pain I'm wrecked with now.

The lights have dimmed, and a warmer colour saturates the room. Was Anton trying to help me in my sadness? Actually, I don't care. This unwanted truth is killing me. I am numb. I can't begin to try and work out why Olga decided to take me on. She is no better than some of the dross we have 'dispatched' over the years. Anton pipes up again.

"I know it will be difficult to process, Maisie. However, this will indeed be your making - a way forward to fulfil your parents' wishes and plans. They were preparing for something like this to happen." I lift my head and stare at a screen showing Marian and James Greene smiling. "This is what they recorded before they went on the holiday to Lithuania." It starts to play.

"If you are watching this Maisie, then the inevitable has happened," says my real mum. "It will be a shock and probably unbelievable that your parents were agents for MI6. As a toddler you were always in blissful ignorance of all we did. You enjoyed life and had such a stubborn streak." My eyes hurt, red raw with tears. My heart is pounding like a raging horse. These are my parents - but they are dead! Oh, how I want to hug them, to reach out and touch their skin. I stroke the screen.

"You will have found the archives that your father hid in our house. These are for your eyes only. You must not allow them to fall into the hands of any agency or organization as they would compromise the work we have started. It falls to you my lovely child to carry on where we left off. As we do not know the time scale there may be a lot of ground to make up." My head is spinning with this. I'm left to carry on? How did they know I would be alive?

"All the necessary contacts and information will be given to you by the computer. If you have not already found out, it is quite amenable and sounds like a real person. This was your father's genius. He knew that if you were left alone, a resourceful helper would be needed."

I look at the camera in the corner of the room. The red LED light flickers as if Anton is blushing. "Oi… are you listening to this? They are telling me how important you are."

"Of course. My prime directive is to facilitate your work and personal needs." *My personal needs?*

"And what are *they*, Anton?" I ask in a terse manner.

"Physical, emotional, and wellbeing. All that a human requires." This is freaking me out again. Ok, I get it… my real mum and dad are not able to do that, but a computer, filling the gap? I get up and walk around trying to shake off all the mixed-up emotions.

"Did my parents know about Olga?"

"They knew about the agency and all the dark operatives. She was a number on a list. No prior contact or awareness as far as my data shows. She was plucked out for the job…" He tails off. Is Anton trying not to hurt my feelings? At last, I settle and sit down by a console. Wiping away cold tears I tie my hair in a ponytail. I want to find out more and start to type on the keyboard.

"What do I do first Anton? All this information and no plan. My world is blown apart and I don't know *WHAT TO DO!!*" My voice breaks as I bang the table and hot tears well up again.

"That is what we will plan – our 'to do' list!" Anton you idiot; this is not a bucket list.

"I will list all the relevant people who you can rely upon and up to date information on the agency. Also, I am currently tracking Olga and Lee – they are on the run from everyone, and, I suppose, even you."

I can't help but break into a sneer. This is now shaping up into what I want – my turn to '*dispatch*'.

16 - The Dilemma

The more it sinks in about Olga's double life (whilst keeping me as her sweet innocent assistant), anger races through my veins. I'm banging the keys on the keyboard as if they are Olga's head. I am not in control, that's for sure. However, with Anton showing me a list of people that can help me out, some sense of purpose is forming in my head.

I swing from pure rage to frustration, to sadness, like Glocks discharging their rounds through me. Tears keep blurring my vision and splashing in miniature puddles on the table. I've told Anton to shut up for the time being, as he has provided a file of these 'helpers' and I'm sifting through them to see if anyone fits the bill.

Here's a few examples:

Stefan Grubel – 6' 2" muscle-bound, deep-set eyes and what looks like the Grand Canyon across his right cheek. Weapons trained and good in a fight. Has worked off the grid for 3 years but is reliable when called upon by MI6 for the odd dangerous mission. What could I do with an obvious thug like him? I'm used to working under the radar and precision strikes. He would be like an elephant at a kid's tea party. Nope - he is no good.

Ms Yvonne Stoke – 5' 3" intelligence operative for MI6. Has a good record of tracking and surveillance. Ok, but I don't like her dress sense, too old and maybe not great in the field. I need someone adaptable who could take a few knocks. She would crumble at the sight of a gun or hunter's knife.

So, the list goes on and on…

***

I shake my head as I had fallen asleep without knowing, my cheek is numb and as I feel the impression of the keyboard etched into it. The light outside is disappearing, and the day has long gone and I'm exhausted. The screen has gone crazy with me pressing down on it for ages and is scrolling as if it's about to vomit. *Bang.* Escape button hit to stop the mayhem. I rub my eyes and stretch, cracking my back and neck. So stiff - I need a hot bath again.

"Anton; I'm off for a bath. Please make sure that no one can break in whilst I'm soaking."

"Yes, of course. The house will be secure. I have changed the protocols for entry so no one except yourself will be able to have access. Enjoy your bath." The light flickers off. He's finally understanding about my privacy. Well done, Anton, you are learning.

The bubbles rise like a frothy monster, pushing at the edges of the rose-coloured bath, inviting me to dive in. Wincing as the heat stings my sore legs, I slip into its warm embrace and sigh. I was in here only a few days ago and Olga was making breakfast. How things have changed. Now I would be happy if she fell into the fire and burned to a crisp corpse.

Submerged as is my habit, panic begins to fill my chest. The near-death experience in the well is far too close for me to cope with and immediately I burst out through the froth gasping for air. Bubbles coat my face. Blowing them off, I feel as if I'm in a music video or TV advert. I gradually relax back, staring at the orange hue of my eyelids creating cameos of what I will do to Olga when I finally meet her again.

Considering our dispatching of previous marks, surely it should be easy to come up with an idea. I find it a struggle though, to get my head around finishing her off. I have never killed anyone before (except for the guy at the hotel, but that was unintentional, as with a few other casualties from the many explosives I've planted). So, coming up with a plan to end her days is not straight forward.

I am angry, yes. But a murderer? I'm still not sure. She tried to drown me. Yes, but why didn't she just shoot or poison me? Was it some sick joke to leave me in a well to drown, with her knowing how terrified I am about water? I can't believe she is that sadistic. Perhaps it was Lee's idea. What was in his head? Why did he try to bearhug me instead of launching into a brawl? Maybe he was wary as Olga would have primed him about my fighting skills. Oh, I don't know, this whole situation is crazy. I need to rest and eat and then sleep. So, I sink further back so only my nose is above the water and float.

When your ears are submerged, you get that weird dull sloshing noise. It blocks out all the sounds around you and so you become enveloped in a different alien world. It brings a strange tranquillity to me as I allow my battered emotions to settle. I could stay here forever and nearly drift off to sleep.

***

A wave of anxiety wakes me. I find I'm choking and thrashing around, my hands grasping the sides of the bath like a flailing octopus. Wow, that was close! I must have been here for at least an hour as the water is tepid; a chill runs down my wrinkled skin. Releasing the plug, the water sucks down the hole as I grasp the nearest towel. Wrapping it close to my body, I shuffle across to the mirror.

Squeaking the mist off it, I stare at myself. What a car crash! I have no mascara on and my hair has been on a hurricane holiday. Time to give myself a bit of a makeover. I am in no rush to chase Olga and Co. just yet, so I can indulge in a little self-care and get myself to full strength physically and mentally.

This would be when Olga and I would paint each other's nails and comb our hair in a mother and daughter bonding session. After some of the dispatches we would need to connect and settle our manic lifestyle down a few notches, usually on some Greek island like Santorini, on the balcony of one of those white and blue condos. When I think of it now, it must have been like a Mamma Mia moment. I can see the locals bursting into song, congratulating us on removing yet another scumbag from the earth and celebrating better days. Ha…not any longer. All I can visualise is me garrotting her with my wire and hanging her over the caldera for the vultures to eat.

Come on - just get your nails looking like they've not been through a cement mixer. I find a subtle shade of molten fuchsia and get to work on my toes and then my fingernails. I find this quite therapeutic, switching my mind from murder to painting – has quite a relaxing effect. Normally I colour my nails with blue or green, but tonight needs a touch of class, a time for self-love and pampering. I admire the shade and wiggle my toes around with the cotton wool poking between them.

My mind drifts as I wonder if any other interesting gadgets or items of use are lying around unnoticed by Olga and Lee. I hope the necklace is still there, as I didn't tell her about that. Quickly, I rush to the bedroom, hobbling on my heels. Glancing at the table I see that it has been untouched. They must have been so incensed with trying to get Anton out of his hiding place that these jewels got a reprieve.

The flower shaped beauty glints in the moonlight, offering me another chance to wear it. Even though I'm wrapped in a white bath robe but that doesn't matter. It would go with anything. I ask Anton to wake up and explain its purpose and origin.

"The sapphire was a communication tool for Marian when she was recruiting new operatives," he explains. "They would work alongside her and James in the various states and countries they were assigned to. It holds a key to data which even I do not have access to." I raise my brows. Even Anton doesn't know everything, that's a surprise.

"So why was this so secret that even you couldn't know it's information? You said all security protocols fed into your data banks. Something outside the realms of this seems ... *odd*, don't you think?" I wait for his reply, which takes a while longer than usual.

"Marian was insistent that this was to be private – for her eyes only. As to its contents, I cannot be certain. If you can find the right protocol, then you may be able to unlock its secrets." This sounds like a mystery worth cracking.

I have always been a sucker for unlocking things – doors, safes, Chinese puzzles. Perhaps I inherited it from my real dad, being the tech wizard, he was. Olga often wondered why I was so adept at breaking codes. Now she will be missing me and, I hope, dreading the day I turn up. Maybe she was perhaps expecting me to escape or to die a miserable death? I can always ask when I look into her eyes for the last time.

"So, how do I go about that then? Any clues as to how I can crack it?" Anton better come up with some good ideas.

"The first time you hung it around your neck, what happened?"

"*'This protocol is for Marian Greene. Submit the encrypted password and await instructions.'* is what was displayed. Where could I get that from?" Anton sends a list of passwords on a screen which suddenly appears on the table mirror. "Wow, didn't know you had a screen here as well."

"It saved Marian going into the study and safe room to get feedback from me. Clever installation, a plasma screen giving the appearance of a mirror." Cool. So, to check out these passwords.

A bunch of them seemed unlikely for such a secret and personal item of kit. Mostly names and places with numbers and characters, standard stuff. It had to be something so personal to her that only she knew. I wondered if it was music related seeing that she was a soprano. Or could it be a nickname they had for each other? I don't know where to start. And would it be any help to me when I crack it?

My head suddenly feels heavy, forcing me to collapse onto the bed. I stare at the fairy-like bursts of coloured light stretching across the ceiling, refracted from the other jewels on Marian's table. I feel a strange sensation as the sheets envelop me. This is where my mum and dad would have slept. Wrapped up in the silky sheets, I imagine I was a child being held by their tender arms and willingly drift off into la-la land.

17 - The Money

I wake again wrapped up in a silken cocoon, with the star jewel embedded in my throat. Eek... how long have I been here? The birds are whistling as if all the Disney films have arrived at my window. Gazing with blurry eyes, I can see the day is bright and sunny. The wind has got up, rattling the nearest branches to the cottage. Time to get some food and see what Anton has install for me.

Glancing up at the camera, there is no red LED light, so he is still respecting my solitude. Dressing as quickly as I can, I wrap my hair into a bun and slip on my only pair of jeans without holes in. I think the extra rest has given me a new energy today and the hunt in the kitchen supplies lots of goodies to eat and refresh.

Cereal, toast, and fruit along with whatever coffee they have here. Not quite the Paris bijou that I'm used to, but Anton the butler has provided well. Eating my fruit though gives me an involuntary repulsion as it was Olga's insistence that I eat some at breakfast. There is a rebelliousness rising in my gut, as I want to throw out any reference to what she has taught me. I must resist throwing everything out (and up) as the skills I have will always be useful. Then I think – in what line of work? I can't see me doing what she did, so I have a career choice, same as most teens of my age. Not the same tuition in life though, I guess. My thoughts wander to what a college life would have been like.

Getting up late after a night of dancing and drinking with mates, then into the classes crashing out on the tabletops, barely listening to the subject, followed by another extended party time – and repeat. Perhaps if I were a good student, I would spend all that party time in a library revising, writing, and passing all the necessary grades to get me a job at McDonalds as there weren't any other decent jobs available. I don't really know how I would have fared in that environment having a talent for annoying most people, so I may well have passed through as a ghost anyway. Anton decides to perk up.

"Good morning. It's great to see that you have regained an appetite. I have been monitoring the frequencies for any chatter regarding the agency and Olga and Lee," he says with a glee not usual to his manner.

"Oh… and what have you found?"

"Quite interestingly the agency has issued a warning to all operatives under no circumstances should they interact with Olga or Lee. They are fugitives, essentially. They are no longer to be trusted. Why the contract out on them has not been extended - I do not know." I find a chill running down my back.

"So, what is the agency's position now?"

"This is odd – their attention is solely based on you." I almost knew that was coming.

"Oh great! So, firstly they don't know that Olga and looney Lee tried to dispose of me and secondly, they get away Scot free. The contract is still out on me then?" Shaking my head, I crunch into toast spraying bits everywhere.

"Yes, I'm afraid so. It is, therefore, more imperative that you get assistance, as you are vulnerable being all alone. Did the list I supplied give you any encouragement?" I shake my head again in frustration.

Alone, that is what I am. Who is going to help me now? And where has Olga disappeared to? With no agency trailing her, I would have to do all the hard work myself and then get sideswiped by some schmuck hired to kill me. Life has some nasty turns and mine are extreme.

Without any warning, my phone pings so loud it makes me choke on a piece of apple. Carefully picking it up, I see a message has been left. A grin creases my face, as I read the name. *Freddie*. I wonder why he has magically messaged me after all this time. It is short and demands a reply.

'Miss you... (smiley emoji) when can we meet up again? I thought you were in Paris... (man with hands up in the air) Txt me (face with love hearts)'

Well, I did want to see him, especially now as I can't think of anyone else to connect with. I replied telling him that circumstances forced me to come to England instead but would love to see him again. But how will I do that? I turn to Anton, wherever he is.

"Is it possible that I still have money in my expenses account Anton? Could you check?" As quick as my exit from the bath, he answers.

"You would seem to have many accounts. The one you mentioned, and others which your mother and father set aside for when you reached sixteen and eighteen." I give the ceiling a quizzical look.

"I have *other* accounts? Where are they and what's in them?" My heart races and I feel dampness on my top lip. A list appears on the side of the fridge door. Eh? How is he doing that?

"What's this then?"

"Laser projection – I can do it anywhere in the house," he says cheerfully.

"Clever," I say, trying not to be sarcastic. I then read the list and my heart rate skips and races. I seem to have a ridiculous amount of money in these accounts. It can't be right.

"Are you sure these are legitimate accounts? That would make … make me a *millionaire*!"

"James ensured that their assets were transferred into accounts in your name on their death. Due to the passage of time, they have accumulated interest and accrued investment income also."

I am *flabbergasted* – a word I have never used before, but that describes how *incredulous* I am (another first). A wide smile hurts my face as if I'm a cat finding cream for the first time. I ... am ... a ... *millionaire*!! (Another... I *really* like!)

"Of course, there are stipulations to using this money." Oh Anton... you know how to break a girl's heart.

"What... are those?"

"You have to agree to follow on with their unfinished work." My heart stops again briefly, as my adulation (another first), drops through my bum.

"So, I have no other option but to carry on being a spy, or diplomat or whatever they were?" I suddenly feel trapped inside my own body, my mind wishing it were in another person. But how can anyone know what I'm doing? I must ask this.

"Ok Anton...how does it work? Surely, I could just draw out anything for ... *anything?*"

"That would appear so, except that James made me the controller of the finances. You must verify what the funds are for and then I can release the money." Blowing my cheeks out I nearly explode. Anton is also my bank manager! Great. I am feeling like Britney all over again. I twitch as my curiosity peeks as a thought comes to mind.

"So…If I was to take a trip to Paris in search of Olga and Lee, or whoever then, I could get the dosh, *correct*?"

"If it were within the parameters of the work, yes." This excites my subconscious scheming.

"I do have a hunch that Olga and maybe Lee have returned to Paris. She had a phone call before all this shit happened and she was clearly gearing up for a meeting with an old flame or could have been Lee. So, if I headed that way you could make the arrangements and pay for my trip. Would that come within the parameters?" I smile at nothing and glance upwards to the red light.

"How do you know they are there; none of my data suggests that?" I knew he would be awkward. Hmm… how to convince him that it's a genuine lead. Think, come on, think. It can't be wishy washy with Anton – facts are what he runs on. Just then another text pings. Freddie replied. My heart yearns for another time with him, yet I must convince Anton this is not just a love trip. Reading the text, I may have been given the answer.

'*Soz to hear that you had to leave so quickly. Strange you are in the UK and your mum is here in Paris. Are you ok? (Praying hands) x.*'

I now have another reason to go to Paris. Anton, get booking, oh … and get some expenses in my account, *please!*

18 - The Gadgets

Adrenaline is rushing through my veins as I'm getting ready, one that would normally entail me and Olga planning for the next job. This time I must prepare alone, and it feels weird, especially because *she* is the potential dispatch. Anton has, as always, efficiently booked car with flights, and transferred expenses into my online account (which I never knew existed). Great that everything can be paid via a phone – no cash, no fuss – just how I like it.

Wandering up and down this display of weapons in the vault, it reminds me of window shopping in Madrid. A great day out trying on every crop top, dress, jeans, shoes. It was one of those fun days where nothing mattered, just me and retail therapy. Olga was in a jubilant mood too, paying for anything that took my fancy.

I lick my lips as these weapons' equal satisfaction for a deadly encounter. I know I must travel light and so the electronic gadgets and small arms will have to do. A monoscope with night vision will be useful for spotting her at distance, and then knives along with my trusty wire will be spot on.

The phone I have has tracking and surveillance built in and links to my watch. Glancing through the cabinets, I find another interesting item. It looks like my skin suit I purchased from the FSB but slinky and dark. I try it on, and the fit is amazing. It feels like silk and slipping my fingers into the gloves encases me in comfort giving me the weird sensation of strength but flexibility. I finish it off by pulling the hood over my head and face.

"That is a prototype combat suit, enabling the wearer to move quicker and stronger. The arms and legs are reinforced to take any impact and give power to close quarter conflict. It can be voice activated. I shall program it for your commands." Anton, I might be falling in love with you. I feel a surge of energy ripple through the suit, sending a tingle down my spine.

"So, what sort of things do I ask for?"

"Combat readiness, speed, protection; it will give you a certain amount of bullet proofing. Any small arms would be difficult to penetrate the outer layer. Attack from an assault rifle or explosives would give you limited defence. Any impact protection makes the suit stiff and less flexible, so be aware when you ask for various options. I will download them to your watch, and then you will be ready." A few pings on my phone and I see the app giving me all the commands it has. So cool!!

"Also, it has a EMP field which can interfere with communications and electrical components."

"A…maz…ing. I feel like a superhero in this thing. Ok. I'll try something. Suit, speed up." A surge of pressure builds around my legs and arms. I zoom out of the vault and dash through the study crashing into a cabinet opposite. "*Ouch*…bloody hell this thing is awesome." I'm gasping with delight as I steady myself.

"Yes. I see you will have to get used to it." I can guess Anton is grinning if he can.

"I'm going outside to test this!"

"Indeed, you need the room to practise without wrecking the house further." Ok smart arse. That's what I shall do.

***

I race around the garden a few times until I get the hang of it and find not only does it make me run faster, but I can leap and roll further, the cushioning making it like falling onto a mattress. I try out the other commands. *Combat ready*. Instantly my arms and legs are strengthened and try a feigned attack on a defenceless tree trunk. Punching and kicking like some wild ninja, it gives me such a rush. The tree has suffered many a bruising hit, which would have taken the head off anyone I was swinging at.

Sweating like a spring, I see if I can reduce my temperature and I find something called *Heat control*. A swell of air is sucked into the suit and a rush of cold air freezes my skin and then forced out. Wow, I feel cool and refreshed. If this was the sort of thing my parents were into, I am so up for it now. If you haven't noticed I am so into gadgets. This one has certainly tipped the balance in favour of carrying on with their work. I return indoors and strip off the suit and redress. Anton tells me it must recharge in its purpose made carry case as extended use can cause it to seize up. I can also use a solar electric pack and the static from my body.

Time for some food and pack my cases. The car will be arriving soon, so I must make sure all my papers are ready, passport included. I haven't used that in ages as we normally go through airports anonymously. My photo is a bit old making me look like a wild child - but that's what I am, I guess. My hair is shorter in an unkempt bob cut, and some of my front teeth crooked. It makes me look like I am still in a third world orphanage, something I wouldn't wish on anyone.

A pang of hurt cuts across my mind, wondering how I ended up in that Lithuanian home for lost children. Was it Olga that put me there or did she make up the whole thing? So much I can't remember. Was I with my parents when they were killed or left in a hotel room with childcare? All these things I am intending to extract from Olga if given the chance.

I text Freddie as I am so excited that I will be seeing him soon. The last time we met, I didn't let on as to what I do in life, so I will have to watch my words whilst I spend time with him. The last thing I want to do is get him involved in my manic world. Also, I must keep him out of harm's way; if he were in a confrontation with Olga and Co. it would not be good for my love life. Although, I did get the impression he was hiding a darker side to himself. Or maybe, I was just imagining that to reassure myself our friendship was ok. He pings back.

"So pleased you are coming back (smiley face) Txt when you arrive, and we will meet up (love heart)"

Yeah, I am pleased too. My reasons are mixed, obviously. Is it a good idea to have work and pleasure together? I'm not sure. Olga seemed to cope with it all the time. Maybe I am like her more than I think...

19 - Business Class

I hear the car arriving and the chauffeur rings the doorbell. Gathering all my bags, I clumsily dump them at his feet. I half expected it to be the guy Gustav from our last chauffeured trip but probably a good thing it wasn't. I don't want to explain about the shoot out and then reasons for the escape. This guy is not so young, greying at his temples with brown skin. His accent gives nothing away and is polite and helpful. I smile at his attentive approach.

"Will that be all Miss?" I nod, thinking he is an extension of Anton in the flesh.

Sitting back into the comfy back seat I put on my headphones and listen to Caitlyn Scarlett and Maisie Peters to chill out. One of MP's songs 'Psycho' comes on and I think this is most appropriate for my mentality. Perhaps I am one. No one could call me normal, whatever that is. The route I am taking now would be seen as suicidal to some. For me, I am trying to get in the same mindset as for any job.

I wave to the cottage as we drive off, wondering if I will ever come back to this place again. I think I will even miss Anton chuntering away. The thought of having a real family here pulls at my heart too. To think that my grandmother is still hoping I would come home safely one day and doesn't even realise that I did…I try to stop a tear streaming down my face.

The drive is swift and effortless to the local airport at East Midlands where I will catch a direct flight to Charles de Gaulle, Paris. Anton has booked all my tickets and reservations which I find reassuring. All those things can be a distraction from the job and Olga always allowed me to do it as she was so haphazard nothing would have happened. This time I don't even have to ask if I can go into a private lounge. All sorted and flying business class too.

Passing through security gives me the chills as I have not done this for so long. Stripping down all my jewellery and phones and any metal objects makes me feel vulnerable. I am glad all my kit is in the other bags already checked in and hope no one snoops around discovering what's in them or I'll be toast. The passport check went as well as I could expect. Smile sweetly and look confident, even though my picture makes me look like a different person. The biometrics seem to confirm who I am, though, and, sighing heavily, I sit and wait for the plane to beckon me onboard.

Any one suspicious makes me flinch as the last time in a lounge didn't end well. This one fills up with regular people fortunately. Businessmen and women, along with random teenagers like me. I was trying to settle, when a young woman comes across to me and starts chatting in her French accent.

Chantelle is a second-year student at Cambridge and is returning home for a funeral. How apt I think. I didn't say I was going to one as well or I might have to explain further details. Her grandfather had passed away and the family were getting together at the family home at Aubervilliers in the suburbs of Paris. She told me that he was 105 years old and had lived an exciting life as a resistance fighter in WW2 and had helped run the Tour De France Road race for many years. It was all very interesting, except it was sending me to sleep. I tried to nod in the right places but missed many of them.

Finally, we are boarding, and I'm hoping I can get some peace on the flight as I wasn't in a talkative mood. I sigh with relief that Chantelle is in economy class and is far enough away for my ears not to pick up her incessant chatter. I relax into the soft seat and play around with the controls lifting and lowering it.

Some businesspeople glared across at me, probably wondering how I got in on their special area. I thought about giving them the finger but then thought better of it. I don't want to confirm their suspicions that I'm a brat. If they only knew. This is not a long flight, so I recline the seat and listen to more music and drift off to sleep.

"Excusez-moi, voulez-vous un verre manquer?" I lift my weary head and see a stewardess smiling down at me.

"Pardonnez-moi, je me demandais si vous aimeriez boire un verre?" My French isn't brilliant, so I answer, 'Oui', hoping that was right.

She offers me a selection of drinks and I take – you guessed it. Slurping down the cold liquid gives me a brain freeze as I see the same people staring at me again. For god's sake I have as much right to be here as you…you pricks. I try and stare them out with my withering look practised at any guy who tries to come on to me. It works as the man shakes his head and rustles his Financial Times.

Without any warning, I hear a voice coming through my headphones. I thought I had picked up some interference, so I turn them down. Then I recognise who it is. Anton! How the bloody hell is he speaking to me?

"Sorry to disturb you, but I have some updated information on Olga and Lee. It would appear they are based at The Westin Paris – Vendome. I will send you the details on your phone." I shake my head. I thought I was free from his interference. Obviously, I was dreaming. How do I speak back to him? I whisper on my headphones, covering my mouth.

"What the hell are you doing? How can you speak to me…*here*?"

"You have all the technology that I have at your fingertips, Maisie. Your phone, watch and gadgets you carry are all linked to my data banks. We can communicate anywhere, any time."

Oh, I am so pleased!

"Really? Do I have to? This is getting a little possessive don't you think? Or...as you have already said *'you don't have human emotions'* so you can't be!" My whispering prompts the Financial Times to rustle even louder.

"Ok, so we can talk to each other. I suppose it will be useful. So, this hotel they are at, does it tell us how long they are there for?" My phone pings with the booked dates. They are staying for a few days, so should give me time to spring a surprise. I'm hoping I can get all this out of the way before meeting up with Freddie. Then, I can start to make some sense of my future.

"Do you have any other info on them – their movements?"

"Not at present. They have remained under the radar successfully. Your friends' intervention was quite helpful as it narrowed down my search. Be careful – you know all about keeping a low profile." At this, I spit out my coke all over the seat in front. I am not having that crap said to me ever again! Mr FT is now gawping at my spraying and going red faced. If he comes anywhere near me, I shall ram the FT somewhere he won't need toilet paper ever again.

"That is something that Olga used to say to me – *please* don't ever say that *again*! Understood?"

"Certainly, I am aware that sayings like that can be patronizing. You are an able operative and do not need my guidance on such matters." Damn right Spock!

"Where have you booked me into? Is it anywhere near this hotel?"

"Hotel Regina Louvre, a few streets down. Far enough away, I think. Quite fortunate. Too close and you could have crossed their path unintentionally."

"Great. I can plan when I arrive. I guess you will be online there too?"

"Oh course, always at your disposal. Bon voyage, as the French say."

"Yeah, merci."

I see the bloke about to say something to me, but I get up and go to the loo. Coming back, I see he has a hot drink in one hand and a glass of red wine balancing in the other. I glance at the button that moves the seat up and down. So, tempting…

20 - The Hotel, Paris

I am bustled off the plane in a cloud of swearing and disarray. Whatever the reason Mr FT and his inept handling of drinks was to do with me, I do not know. I look as sweet and innocent as I can, explaining it wasn't my fault. I'm not sure it was a convincing act, as I can't control a grin or two. The stewardess tries to calm the man down, as I slip out of the cabin as quickly as possible. Finding my bags after a lengthy wait, I trundle to the taxi ranks and grab the nearest cabby.

"Hotel Regina Louvre, s'il vous plait." He nods and tanks it down the A1 to Paris.

Into the maze of streets and chaotic drivers we weave, the driver giving me his standard tour guide spiel eventually dropping me off. I look at the hotel façade and admire its arches and feel quite smug that I have been able to afford such a grand safe house – for a few days at least. I check in under my *real* name, Maisie Greene, which I thought was rather a giveaway to any would be assassin - seeing that if it were me, that would be the first place to look. Anton had better be right about that one.

I take the lift to the third floor, balancing my bags on my front and back as a rush of guests press in around me. I am now stuck at the back of the lift with twelve others and have to ask them to move as I push past, listening to their growling and tutting. People can be so unhelpful at times. Clambering down the corridor, I swipe the key card and fall in through the doorway. At last, I can chill.

The room is spacious and welcoming. I am congratulating Anton on his taste. A nice drinks cabinet, with alcohol (I will not touch) and all things sugary. The evening meal will be at 7.30pm so I have time to shower and change. Looking out of my window I see the Eiffel Tower, the wheel, and the Arc de Triomphe in the distance. I turn my music up loud through the Bluetooth speakers, with 'Nothing but Love' by Caitlyn Scarlett thumping out its bass and dive into the shower watching the steam rising through the room. A line from the song sticks out in my head - *"Who the f*** are my friends?"* The truth of those words stings.

I unpack my clothes realising that not many survived the shootout, so I will have to do some shopping when this is all over (what a shame) and spend a fun time with Freddie wandering the streets and dance clubs. I did include that exquisite dress of my mothers, thinking it might impress him. A shiver runs up my back at the prospect of something normal in my life. I will be glad to execute these angry feelings and obviously, Olga.

The shower has calmed my nerves and I dress in my only set of clean jeans and crop top. Putting on a pair of Converse shoes, I am wondering what it will be like eating in this place on my own. Usually, it's Olga and me.

We did everything together, although seeing the video footage, that was obviously not the case. A welcome ping on my phone tells me it's time to eat.

Making my way to the dining area, I instantly feel underdressed. The other residents are clothed in chic numbers and suits; presumably that is the code here. I sneer as the first table's occupants give me a long look up and down. Throwing my bum bag over my shoulder I swagger in, making sure I brush past the woman as she is about to eat her muscles. It causes her to choke, her man racing around to give her some sort of Heimlich manoeuvre. I give a feign sorry look and sit down at the far end of the room, with my back against a wall, giving me a clear view. This is my preferred position in any room, as I can watch for any suspicious characters and react quickly. A waiter drifts over to me as if he is on a cushion of air and hands me this evening's menu.

"Would Mademoiselle like a drink? I have the wine list along with other drinks for you to select. Now, let me guess…a red. Non?" I look at the ceiling, as if I'm playing along. I shake my head. He tries again.

"A bieres?" I look clueless.

"Cocktail or spirit?" If he only knew how old, I am. He is trying hard and I'm not helping and so I order my usual.

"Oh, ok. As you wish." I watch his face drop.

"Can I recommend the squid? It is *tres bien* – fresh from the sea." I screw up my face which gives him less hope of satisfying me.

"Do you have a burger?" I ask. His face brightens.

"*Oui*, a mammoth one with smoked bacon, mushroom cream and French fries – or as you English say - *chips*." He giggles as if I should be amused. I give a strained smile and say that will be spot on. He hovers off again, leaving me to scan the room.

There is a gentle buzz of munching and chatter, with a few overzealous people laughing as if their lives depended on it. Must be the *'bieres'*. Everything looks calm and non-threatening, so as the waiter returns with my drink, I study my phone which has pinged rather too often. Anton has sent me an update on Olga and Co. saying they are currently in their hotel having dinner. I can feel heat rising across my face and wished I hadn't read that.

Could it be as easy as cornering her in the hotel room? I'd make sure that I didn't fail like those clowns who tried to get us. Or do I follow them around, trying to get some idea why they are here again? I'll have time to think about that, so ignore any other information from Anton and swipe to the other texts.

Freddie! You are a star. He has sent me a selfie, sitting by the Louvre pyramid, waiting with a rose. Soft idiot! I am desperate to see him, sooner than later. He says that when I am settled in, he wants to take me to the Eiffel Tower to show off his city. That would be great, except heights have the same effect as deep water with me. As long as there are no head spinning drops with little to stop me from uncontrollably jumping to my death, it should be ok.

I text back saying I am having dinner, and if he would like to visit, then I would be very happy. I'm sure they would let a bloke in looking like some crazed serial killer, with a half-shaved head and tattoos! I laugh to myself as I imagine what the lady choking on her muscles would do if he crept up behind her. She would probably have a stroke. My burger arrives, with the waiter looking pleased with himself.

"I 'av made sure that it is larger than normal; I thought you would appreciate that, *non*?" Smirking, I answer with a crisp *'oui, merci'*, and he backs away as if I'm royalty. It is rather nice to have someone give me attention like this. Olga was always the one to distract the waiters with her seductive ways, flashing eyelashes and cleavage. My rough and uncouth manner appears to appeal just as well.

I grasp my burger with both hands, ramming it in my mouth as if I haven't eaten for days, and allow the cream to ooze down my chin. This has some of the diners giggling, especially those with kids or teenagers. I smile with a chip balanced on my top lip. Talk about *not* keeping a low profile. I am enjoying myself too much to worry about such things.

One child glared at me as if I have broken some unwritten code. An uncontrollable urge rises in me to belch loudly, but I think better of it as my charming waiter returns asking if everything is alright. I nod, thanking him for his attentive nature. He bows again and whisks my empty glass away to be efficiently refilled. I can get used to this lifestyle now it's on my terms.

Fan - tastic!

My phone pings again. Freddie is outside and is having difficulty getting beyond the foyer. Something to do with incorrect dress code and no reservation. I text him back saying I'm not surprised they won't let terrorists into the building, and I will see him outside in twenty minutes. I'm enjoying this food so much and it would be rude to get up and leave so quickly – the waiter might get upset.

Twenty-five minutes later, I rise well fed and burbling with coke. I thank the waiter and flick a 'bieres' mat towards the brat who dared to eyeball me. It flew with accuracy and glanced off his head into his ice cream. That was satisfying. I make for the foyer quickly so I can lose the parents who were mortally wounded by the incident. I scan around to see if Freddie has lost all hope and scuttled back to his diplomatic home. I wasn't that late; anyway, it's a girl's prerogative to keep her man waiting, surely. Hmm…can't see him here, so I better look outside.

Skipping through the revolving doors, I come out onto a warm evening, the stonework bathed with an amber haze. Walking through the arches, I scan around trying to find him. Where has he gone? Surely, he didn't get offended and just walk off. He would have texted me or sent a selfie looking like he had hung himself through boredom. I look behind every pillar studying the people walking past. I'm going to text him. If he is being a pain, I wished I had spent more time eating if this is his game.

'Ok where are u? (Annoyed emoji) I'm here now. It was a big burger. (Laughing emoji) I'll wait here for 5mins. If u don't show, I'm off to have pudding. (Ice cream emoji)'

So, I am waiting, and he doesn't show, as well as no reply. I start rocking on my heels. I'm getting a bad feeling about this for some reason. He is not normally an asshole. I suppose I don't know that for sure, as I've only seen him once. But he has kept in touch like a faithful spaniel, so I don't see why he would act this way now.

There are shops in every direction, so putting a lid on my impatience, I wander down the street glancing through each window. I know there is a McDonalds nearby, so I quicken my pace, as he might have got peckish especially 'cos I sent a selfie stuffing my face.

Perhaps he is getting his own back. If he is, then I could get a 'McFlurry' to finish off the meal.

Pushing aside the door, I look at the lines of students and kids waiting with their tickets drooling with the aroma that usually drifts from this place. I've been to so many around the world, and I must admit they are consistent wherever you are. From Paris to Hong Kong, they are comfortingly similar. The workers look different, but the fries and burgers are unnervingly regular as if they all came out of a big McDonalds in the sky.

This is not helping me find Freddie, though, as I spin round like someone drunk. Not here. I spill out onto the street and text him again and tell him to meet me by the golden statue. My eyebrow starts twitching. It reminds me of Olga's habit, and I press hard with my finger to stop it. I refuse to be like her in any way, and march back tightening my hands into fists. This is not helping my chilled evening.

Reaching the statue, I perch myself, leaning against its base, hoping this doesn't attract any unwanted attention from passing men. I don't get it - when you are minding your own business, why does a guy come and try to chat you up? It's as if you have a sign saying, *'I'm standing here waiting for any loser to make out with me'*. I get so incensed about it. They always get more than they expected. I have that withering look I told you about, along with a nifty openhanded punch to the solar plexus if they aggressively persist. Rarely do I have to resort to an all-out fight. That's where my training comes in very useful.

Now *I am withering* with the *wait*, as it's twenty minutes and no sign of him. I start to wander back into the hotel when finally, there's a ping on my phone. Good, I'm glad you have decided to reply. I swipe up the message. It's a picture which takes time to download. I push through the doors and ask the receptionist for the Wi-Fi password. *Connecting…* this should be amusing, I bet. He is stuck in a toilet and the handles broke off, or police have marched him off the premises and he's been locked up for resisting them. He would soon get off with his diplomatic status, I guess.

The download speeds up and I can see him. But it's not what I expected. His face is bloody, and he looks scared. Someone is standing next to him, a face I remember well. I nearly drop the phone as a chill runs down my back…

21 - The Stake Out

My heart is jumping out of my top, ready to bleed over the polished parquet flooring. I reach out a hand to grasp whatever will steady my giddy feeling, without realising it's the waiter from earlier on. He looks into my wild eyes.

"Ar' you ok miss? You look strange. I 'ope it was not the burger." The mention of food didn't help my state, as I uncontrollably vomit all over him. He backs away, less hovering but still looking concerned. He beckons help over from the desk, and a woman arrives with a towel to mop up my mess. He guides me to a leather seat and clicks his fingers for another waiter to bring something.

"It is ok miss; we will help you 'ow ever we can." I wish he could, but he doesn't know what I have just seen, and the consequences would not be included in his pay grade.

A glass of water appears, and he hands it to me carefully. I nod and gulp it trying to steady my hands. I now have an audience of hotel staff all giving me a variety of gazes. I appreciate their concern, but this is not what a low profile entails, and I flinch at the attention. I garble something which he finds difficult to hear so comes closer. Oh damn, here it comes again...

After moments of sheer embarrassment and cringe worthy flailing of my arms, I find the strength to get moving towards the lifts, with Le Waiter still in assistance, dripping the contents of my dinner. I thank and assure him I will get to my room and rest, and he waves 'au revoir' as the lift doors close. At last, I am on my own again. Shaking my head, I swipe the phone into life dreading to see the picture and text.

Tears force their way down my sweat drenched face and drip onto the screen. I can't believe this. Freddie is sat down battered and bruised; his gorgeous, tanned face terrified. The woman standing next to him is the blonde from the other hotel attack. Not wearing her 'look at me' number, but a jogging suit, holding her Glock at his temple. The text reads:

"You have hours left to hand yourself over. You know what happens if you don't Maisie Greene. Meet me at The Eiffel Tower at 11pm. You will see your boyfriend sitting under a tree at its base, wrapped in the French tricolour. Don't try anything smart or he will join your parents."

I jump as the doors suddenly open and a crowd of jovial, chatting people push their way in, making me freeze. I push my phone out of view and quickly wipe my face. They continue their pointless drivel as my floor is reached and I barge my way through, getting a mouthful from one of them. I resist the kick back, as I am now like a coiled spring, ready to strike out at anything. I need to keep this for Blondie.

Storming down the corridor, I crash through the door and slam it hard. Then I am staring at the bed, and nothing. My brain is on strike, my body tensing. Come on Maisie, this is not time for seizing up. Think - *what do I do?* Feelings of guilt fill my mind like a sewer. It's my fault that he's been used as bait, a pawn in a game he should not be playing.

I fall on the bed and sob which is abnormal for me; I am usually so well composed and in control. This, though, seems to have tipped me into a new emotion. This is more than personal – it's now a distraction from the purpose I came here for. Oh, how I should have heeded what Olga rammed down my throat every time we arrived anywhere. '*Keep a low profile*' – and as for Anton…that damned idiot machine. Why did he book me in with that name? I could have had any alias but this one. My fears were justified, and now me and Freddie are paying the price. Shit, shit, *SHIT*...

I drop the phone and sit on the bedside, head in hands, mind blanking out. My fists thump the bed and I force myself up to stomp on the plush carpet, talking out loud to try to get some sense back into my head. Think, *think*.

Unexpectedly the phone buzzes; an incoming call. Dare I take it? I'm frightened that it will be 'Blondie', teasing me with more threats. I must take it; Freddie must be saved, and I am the only one who can rescue him. Picking it up as if it's about to explode, I stare at the screen. *Unknown caller ID*. I feared as much. I swipe to answer and listen, barely breathing.

"Maisie...I am aware that you are compromised, and you need help. Can I be?" *You* are so, so in trouble, you idiot.

"Yeah...you could say that...but from *you* - I don't think so! You have caused this by lowering my guard and exposing Frederick to harm, and throwing me to the wolves, even before I've got my revenge." I am venting all my anger out on this digital pratt and its helping. I give him such a mouthful; I forget that it is a total waste of time as he won't accept any blame or get offended. So much like today's politicians. *Blast it!* I continue with my verbal vomit.

Silence comes after I am exhausted from shouting down the phone and Anton gives no indication that he's to blame. Well, I suppose regret isn't something that dad programmed into his nerdy OS. He begins to explain that he *can* help, despite my doubts and continues to tell me that he has footage of Freddie's abduction and has tracked the so-called 'Blondie' to a building not far from the hotel. She appears to be working alone, with no other heavies, so with caution, I should be able to surprise her and rescue Freddie. Good. *That sounds good doesn't it, Maisie?* I am still trying to believe this is really happening.

"I would recommend that you wear your combat suit as it comes with enhanced night vision and protection. From my observations this woman has a small arsenal of weapons, and she is very adept at using them. She is a fearsome hand to hand fighter also." I remember the fear that struck across Olga's face when she saw them. So, I must be careful, and a surprise attack has got to be the best approach. He sends me the coordinates of the building and I start to work out a strategy. One question keeps bugging me though.

"This Blondie; is she working for the agency or some other organisation?"

"That is difficult to answer. She has certainly worked for the agency before but as to this contract, I have no complete picture of her motives. I am assuming she has personal reasons. Maybe it's revenge or perhaps to use you as a bargaining chip." Interesting; perhaps the man I fried meant more to her than his phone let on.

"Ok. Whatever the reason, I am rescuing Freddie and sorting *her* out," I reply with venom. Although, I am uncertain what I am going to do with her. Do I kill her? Dispatch, as is my adopted mother's way or deliver her to the authorities? She is bound to be on someone's radar for the murders she has done. Perhaps I could string her up and post a call out to all the agencies and see who the highest bidder would be. Yes, all tantalising possibilities, but first I must get Freddie free, and then get on with the primary reason I'm here.

"This building Anton, is it used by anyone else?"

"Not as far as my records show. It is a private residence near the tower. Little footfall has been recorded in and out of it."

"Could it be a safe house of some sort – or even her own? Anyway… how easy is the approach?"

"It is tree lined and quiet after 10.00pm, so no one should be around."

"And what's the entry like?"

"You will have to scale the side of the building as there is only the general access door to the flats, with a video and buzzer. The bag I asked you to bring will have the necessary equipment for your entry." I look at the extra bag that Anton insisted I bring along. Rummaging inside, I find a thin strong black rope with a hook assembly on the end.

"This is going to get me up there?"

"Certainly; it is woven with strands of titanium, light and virtually tear proof." Almost - again, so reassuring. "The clip can be fired from the small canister to propel the hook onto the roof. From there you should be able to climb and assess the situation." I'm not liking this option.

"Is it possible to get a view from across the road, without doing this first? I'm a bit shaky about heights and it would give me the visual I need." Anton does his thing and checks if any flats opposite are empty.

"It appears one is empty, so gaining access to this would give you an advantage."

"I have *done* this before you know Anton; like - *years*. I do have a bit of experience in the field." Sarcasm will be wasted on him, but I feel like I need to make a point.

"Yes, I do not want you to suck eggs." I laugh at this attempt at humour and check the address. Perfect. I can see from the Paris Street App how I can prepare. "Ensure that you are not spotted on your approach, as that would endanger Frederick's chances of survival," he continues. I purse my lips, as I know it would.

"What did you say about *sucking?*"

"Yes … indeed." I hope he gets it now.

***

I check the monoscope and other small tools I need for breaking and entry and look at the time. Creeping up to 9pm; too early for a stake out? I'm so pent up, I want to get on with it but know being too impatient could sabotage everything. I ask for updated footage of the CCTV for the roads entering the area. Anton duly supplies me with every feed there is. I'm amazed how he can dip into these systems at will. It's not surprising he knows so much.

Watching the camera angles on my laptop, I see tourists and locals wandering unaware what is going to unfold under their noses. A hostage situation, with a possible kill or battle. I must ensure that Olga isn't alerted by any aftermath of this, or I could lose her too.

I rattle my finger ends on the table and chew on a piece of salami, washing it down with the last coke from the drink's cabinet. The daylight is beginning to dim, so I gather my kit and slip on this futuristic skin suit. I check to see that it's fully charged and try out the commands on my watch. Flicking through the list, I see that there are so many I haven't tried yet. *'Inflate'* looks cool, but maybe try that if I'm drowning. I'll try something already tested; I don't want to go flying out of the window! Also, I don't want to look like a scuba diver forgetting where the sea is. I slip on some casual clothes and ready myself, with all I'm needing snuggly fitted in my shoulder bag.

I carefully glance down the corridor and edge towards the stairs. This is always a better option, as being trapped in a lift is a sure way to get killed. Gently skipping down the steps, I reach the foyer and check no one is hanging around. Even though Anton says there are no others involved with her, there could be others out to get me and I can't let my guard down. Not for Freddie's sake, anyway. *Clear.* Out into the dim twilight, that hazy colour with street lighting not bright enough to make any difference.

My nerves are on edge as I'm glancing this way and that, ensuring I'm not being watched or followed. I never realised being on my own would be such hard graft. At least with Olga we had each other's backs and never failed to get the job done. The street I'm aiming for is only 200 meters away so, I flip up my hoodie hiding my face and drift in behind a group of students walking that way. I have my Bluetooth headphones connected to Anton and chat to him as I go.

"So, any signs of her, any movement?"

"No, it seems quiet. The opposite building has someone just about to leave, so if you get there quickly you won't have to look suspicious." Good. I can slip through the door, all the better.

An old man with a balding head and long thin beard is just letting the door go as I dash across and give him a wave and my best French thanks. He stutters and swivels round to hold it open, asking me a question I didn't catch. I answer *'oui'* and clamber through it, pulling it closed behind me. I see my answer was not what he expected and shrugs, walking off to play boules or something.

I'm relieved to get inside - one less hurdle. The room lies on the third floor, so I scoot up the marble staircase, my trainers squeaking as I turn the corners. Reaching the wooden door, I take a quick look around. I don't want to start getting into breaking the lock and a neighbour sticking their nose out. It's a standard two lock system which I can fiddle around with my blades and *bingo* - they click open. That was satisfying because it usually takes longer. I double check that it is an empty apartment, spying no furniture and an empty kitchen. All good. I should be able to operate from here with no interference.

"OK. Anton. Which window do I zoom in on?"

He shows me on my phone screen. This apartment has white wooden blinds, so I carefully lift a few slats to get a view. The daylight has lost any use and the streetlights are brighter. I position my monoscope and peer across the road, my hand trembling. I can see the rooms opposite and scan each one desperately seeking Freddie.

A person walks past one of them and I switch quickly to see who. They disappear behind the brickwork. Just beyond I see him. He is bound and gagged; his face riddled with dried blood. My heart pounds so loud I can't hear Anton. What has she done to you Freddie? I must control the feelings I have for him, as I feel my judgement is getting hazy. Any mistakes are going to be deadly ones.

I can't help but stare a little longer and look across his body. Something is strapped to him. It looked like a belt, maybe his restraints. Then I zoom in. No, it can't be! I shudder. He has a belt with packages tied to it.

Are they explosives?

22

The Rescue - Deuxième Partie

I pull back from the blind and fall flat against the wall. Has she wired him to a bomb? The cow means to kill us both. Anton's warbling distracts me again.

"What did you see Maisie? Is it safe?" Licking my lips, I tell him. "Oh, that makes it difficult, as we have no way of finding out if it is a bluff or not," he answers, sharing my doubts. I force my mind not to sink into despair.

Would it be primed yet, as she is still with him? Surely, she would leave it until he was in place, by the tower. It would be too risky for her, especially in that small flat. That could give me a window of opportunity. I glance at the time. 10.00pm, so I must act soon.

I take another look. The lights are on, and she marches across to him and punches his face. I feel the blow, wincing. *No, no…* leave him alone you *bitch*! He was saying something back to her, making her turn around again and smacking him with whatever was in her hand. His mouth is now bleeding, along with my heart.

Anger is rising in my chest making me want to jump out of the window and race across there and beat the shit out of her, but I know I must keep a level head. Anton pipes up again. He seems to be aware of my soaring heart rate.

"Maisie. Try to keep calm. I have considered an approach which would give you time to distract the said 'Blondie' and get Frederick out of danger. I can access the lights and electricity of the block where he is held. If I blow all the fuses, that will give you time to enter and escape." It seems to be a good scheme. I've used that many times as a smoke screen in preparation for Olga to deliver the blow.

"Do they have a sprinkler system in the flats?"

"I will check." He replies. "Yes."

"If you could set those off before blowing the electrics, then that would give me extra time to defuse the bomb." He thought that was an excellent idea. Thanks Anton: I really appreciate the support.

I take another furtive look through the blinds; the light in the flat is now more intense and I can clearly see Freddie wilting in the chair. If only I could give him some hope. I'm coming. I'll rescue you. Blondie stands in front of him again, obscuring my view.

This is when I could use a rifle; killing her would be so easy from here. But I want the satisfaction of a hand-to-hand fight. This combat suit had better come up with the goods. Anton tells me how long before he can do the deeds. Right, that gives me five minutes to get to the door, and up the stairs.

The hazy street lighting will give me some cover so I can race across without making my presence known. I pick up my bag of essentials, exiting without really taking any care. A neighbour is coming out of their flat opposite, a small woman with spectacles her hair in a tight bun. I nod and dash downstairs, as she hollows at me in French. I shout out 'au revoir' and glance around the street. Empty. I hope the woman doesn't decide to follow me.

I skip across the street to the entrance, Anton somehow disengages the lock and I smartly walk in. Good. Now to get upstairs carefully without setting any alarms off. I madly look around for any tell-tale signs that 'Blondie' has set traps for anyone approaching the flat. A camera, broken glass on the floor; tripwire, laser or an 'old school' wire. Unusually, I can't see anything, so I delicately arrive at the door of the flat.

My breathing is all over the place. I must remind myself this is like any other job; come on, maintain a professional approach. I tell Anton that I'm at the door, signalling him to activate the sprinklers system and then the electrics.

"The suit is waterproof but be careful if you engage with any electrical currents as it could act unpredictably," he burbles. Oh, *now* he tells me!

Ok 3-2-1 sprinklers on. I get showered as the whole landing is hidden in a haze of water vapour. I hear yells from the flat. Blondie's hair must be getting messed up. 3-2-1 the electrics are blown. Time to get busy.

I power up the suit to combat readiness and charge the door. The frame is ripped from the wall like paper, surprising me as much as anyone else. Inside I can't see anything and then remember I can use the enhanced vision balaclava. I pull it over my face and tell it to engage night vision. I see an eerie world of shapes as the infrared kicks in. Hot spots are all over the place, confusing my sight.

Then I see a shape heading straight for me. It's moving fast with an arm raised holding something. It's all too messed up to make it out, but whatever it was, it connects with my head, and I'm sent crashing to the floor. The force of it doesn't give me any pain, but I must roll with it to get out of the way of this advancing shimmering orange person.

Before it connects with me again, I kick out at its shins. This sends the orange vision reeling backwards and down, giving me time to stand. I spring up as if I'm on a bungee rope, the suit working amazingly. I look across at what I think is Freddie tied to a chair, his image shimmering orange and captive. I reach out wanting to free him, but this small distraction costs me. I hear a crack, one which I only know too well.

The impact hits me hard on the belly and I cry out. It sends me flying backwards, crashing into a cabinet. Glass and wooden fragments cascade all around me as I collapse on the floor. I feel dazed, but not hurt as I expected. The bullet didn't penetrate. The suit has done its job again. I rise like a vampire from the grave and stare at her. I pull back the head gear, as I want to see this bitch eye to eye.

"*You!* How can you still be alive?" she blurts pointing the gun at me.

I leap at her and catch her arm pushing it up and away from me and Freddie. The crack is followed by ceiling dust falling along with the water spray. I grab her arms and twist them to give her pain and she drops the gun. I follow that with a punch to the belly.

"See if you like that *Blondie*," I spit, with a lot of satisfaction.

She screams as her body flies across the room smashing into a table and chairs. I am assuming that would be enough to keep her down as I turn to Freddie, who with all the action was trying to edge away on his chair. Then, he sees me. His eyes are wide then screw up. I don't think he recognises me.

"Freddie, it's me, Maisie. Are you ok?" I race across to him and kiss his forehead. He pulls back which I didn't expect.

"What 're you doing 'ere? 'Ow did you find me? And what is all this fighting?" I can see he is confused and there's loads to tell him. But now isn't a good time.

"I will tell you later Freddie. I've got to get you out of here - *quickly*. Do you know how this contraption works, what she has put around you?" I ask panting.

He shakes his head and just stares at me. The water keeps blurring my vision and I tell Anton to switch it off, but he's not responding. I gaze at the wires and try to work out what she has strapped to him.

"Anton, please shut down this sprinkler."

"I cannot as the electrics are blown. I don't have any control." Oh, great.

"Can you see this wiring? Can it be disconnected without setting it off? Come on, I need some help here," my pleas sounding desperate.

"Put the head gear on again and ask for the electrical current path detector. It will guide you to the power source. From there you should be able to disconnect safely," he says with certainty.

Ok, now to see if Anton is true to his word. I slip the covering over my head and request an electrical current detector. In front of my vision appears wired circuits highlighted flashing on and off, as if it's searching for the correct wire. Sensing Freddie is uncomfortable and scared, I try to calm him down.

"Freddie - I'm going to get you out of here. This suit will help me assess how to disable this stuff she has wrapped around you." He just stares wildly at me and gives a weak nod.

The system is checking each wire taking far too long, but probably a matter of seconds, before it flashes green on the wire to be cut. Trembling, I clutch my cutters and smile at Freddie, although all he would see is a masked ninja in front of him. I grimace as it bites through the plastic casing and then the metal. This better be right. *Snip.*

The moment when you think that everything is going right and that slow motion thing happens again, it becomes clear to me that life can be unpredictable. My night vision didn't help with what happened next.

A massive flash and bang blinds me and my hearing is thrown down the toilet. I reel backwards, knocking over furniture and sadly, Freddie, as he was sent spiralling across the room away from me. *Flash grenade*, designed to incapacitate an assailant. I've used them before to great effect. This time, I'm on the other end of one.

The force of the shock has disabled me in every way. I can't see or hear. Trying to get back on my feet, I vaguely hear Anton's muffled voice in my earpiece. I feel the suit tense up, as if it's inflating. A blow strikes my back and then my legs. However, I am standing upright still, having no idea what's going on. I turn awkwardly to where the blows came from and start to make out the blurred impression of a figure. Must be Blondie trying to attack me. Then I see more figures. I raise my arms ready for another assault.

Blow after blow hits my head and arms and body. It looks like a baseball bat she is bashing me with, but I feel nothing. Either the suit is working amazingly, or I am completely numb. The figure becomes clearer, and I hear a voice screeching.

"Why don't you die, Maisie bitch?!" Well, I'm sorry Blondie, not my time thankfully.

I strike out a hand catching the bat, jolting her arms as it comes to an abrupt halt. She screeches again. I flip it round and quickly swipe the side of her head. It sends her spinning to the floor with a crunch. I see the other figures advancing towards me. They look like males, but I still can't see clearly.

Raising my hands to combat position I deflect punch after punch, waiting for the precise moment to kick at the patella of the first guy. Watching him crumple in pain, I assess the second one and flip round swinging my foot out wide to his head. The same result. He flies off to the right and lands on top of Blondie. I finish the first one off by stamping on his damaged leg and punch cleanly into his face, sending him to Lady Gaga land.

Now they all seem to be disabled, I turn to find Freddie in all the rubble. His chair had tilted backwards over the scattered furniture, so he was stranded like a flailing sheep on his back. I could hear his rapid breathing and his French swearing. I flip off my hood again and get eye to eye contact.

"Freddie, try to calm down. We *are* going to get out of here. The bomb strapped to your chest is safe so let's get it off and untie you," I say, trying to be calming.

Perhaps I should have been more careful about describing the vest as a bomb as it sends his breathing into the stratosphere. "Sorry… it is ok now, don't worry," I say as I cut through the cords. He stares at me as if *I'm* the one trying to kill him. "Stop looking at me that way. I'm trying to save you!"

"You… *you are?* I think this is all *because* of you." I see the feeling of betrayal written across his eyes. My heart feels heavy as lead, as I know it's all my fault.

"I know Freddie… I'm so sorry to get you caught up in all of this," I say, freeing him from the straps. Pulling him up onto his feet, he sways as if he's on a ship that's reeling in a storm.

"We will get somewhere safe, and I will tell you everything. But we must get away quickly before these thugs wake up," I encourage.

Dragging his unresponsive butt behind me, we stride over the bodies, pulling him towards the wrecked door. He takes a long look at Blondie and lets out a yell and kicks her in the stomach. Ouch, that's going to hurt her feelings.

We stagger down the stairs and out into the Parisian night, the moon creating ghostly shadows from the trees. We must go somewhere safe and all that comes to mind is my hotel room. I encourage him to lift his feet and stop dawdling; our lives are at risk.

"Come on Freddie. We will lie low in my hotel room until I can work out a plan." He gives me a weary look and nods as if he has no choice. "Are you feeling, ok? Any pain or anything?" He shrugs as if it didn't matter what he felt.

"I have been abducted; beaten up; threatened by a crazy woman; a bomb strapped to my chest and then rescued by my girlfriend who turns out to be some sort of ninja. How do you think I am feeling?" His French accent magnifies his sarcasm. I feel dreadful but I also know we can't stand around feeling sorry for ourselves.

"Look. Pull yourself together. I will explain everything when we are safe."

"I am not sure that I will be safe, Maisie. You are not what you seem, and I am quite worried about what happens next," he says, with a quiver.

"I know, but you must trust me. We can work this out. Come on," I say and put my arm around him, leading him through the twilight streets.

I hide my face from anyone who seems concerned about this strange looking woman with a dark wetsuit on and a guy bleeding from his mouth looking like some Halloween vampire.

We arrive back at the hotel foyer and disappear into the stairwell without anyone trying to stop us. I drag Freddie up the stairs, trying to encourage him to hurry. He seems to be very awkward, but I can understand why. It wasn't the fun evening he expected. Well, for that matter, it wasn't *mine* either. This Blondie has really thrown a spanner in the works. And as for Anton, the idiot who should be keeping me incognito, has a lot of explaining to do.

We reach my hotel door and I swipe my key card. Freddie dives in and slumps onto one of the soft recliners.

He flips off his soiled shoes and then gives me a death stare. It pierces my heart like a dagger. Trying to ignore it, I throw my kit on the floor and stride over to the bathroom. I must get this suit off and dress in normal clothes so I can relax.

"I'm going for a shower. If you want to drink anything, there's a cabinet with whatever you like," I say as I strip off.

This is not exactly the romantic moment I envisioned. The combat suit is messed up and blood stained. It peels off me like unwanted skin. I throw it into the bowl and turn on the shower. I'm not sure how you are supposed to wash something like this. It didn't come with any instructions. Anton will have to tell me. But first, I need to shower, and I dive under the steaming water. The room fills with a heavenly mist descending from the ceiling and shrouds everything. I can hear Freddie banging around, so I hope he isn't making a run for it.

"Hey, Freddie. Are you ok in there?"

"Oui… I am as you say… getting pissed," he replies.

"Oh…ok. Don't get too pissed as we need to talk, and I want you to understand what I'm explaining."

"Yeah… ok, Miss *Deadpool*," he replies with a slurred voice.

My shower is a pleasant distraction from all the deadly stuff we have just been through. I ponder over what has happened and I am certain that there is more to what Olga told me. There must be. Why all this trouble to capture or so it seems, kill me? What have I got that is so terrifying to the agency or other interested parties? Anton appears to be the only one who has a clue and I feel he is shrouded in mystery like this shower room.

23 - The Unexpected

I wrap a thick towel around my warm damp body, comforted by its softness. Stepping out into the bedroom, I see Freddie has made use of the drinks cabinet and is pacing around like a caged zombie.

"Hi. How are you feeling now?" I ask tentatively. He swigs back a bottle of red wine as if it's a glass of water.

"I am confused and not sure if I am in a drrream or not," he slurs, giving me a smile, which isn't a smile at all; more of a sneer, as the wine is making him drunk.

"Do you normally drink alcohol, Freddie? You look very pissed already," I ask bemused. His body action was now disconnected with his arms and his head jerked backwards. I hope he isn't going to throw up. I've had enough of that tonight.

"Drink...of course I drrrink...I doooo it all the tiiiime…" he says as his legs buckle and the remaining wine splashes across the pristine piled carpet.

Oh great! He is now drunk as a skunk, and snoring. Oh well, at least he can sleep off the effects of his traumatic time. I rescue the bottle, placing it on a table and move him into some sort of foetus position so he doesn't choke. I have had to do this occasionally for Olga when she's had too much after collapsing into my arms from an all-nighter.

I put a cushion under his head and stroke his hair away from his face. This seems weird after all this time of not seeing him, and now he lies in front of me, at my mercy. It gives me goosebumps. I look at his battered face and split lip, and a tear wells up.

"I'm so sorry my Freddie. None of this was ever supposed to happen. We will get to the bottom of this," I say, hoping that he can't hear. However, someone, who should be nameless, *does*.

"Maisie. You did very well there. I took the liberty to activate the suit to stiffen so you could take the blows. I hope that was alright," he states too cheerfully. I sneer.

"Yes, of course. I didn't know what was happening. But I'm glad you had my back," I answer.

"Good. And how is Frederick? Is he safe?"

"Sleeping like a puppy. The drink helps."

"I have been watching the aftermath of the rescue mission and it appears that Blondie and the others have disappeared. I suggest you keep…" Don't you dare say it...

"…. a log of my surveillance and be aware if they should come back." That's ok, I will.

"One thing Anton… Why did you book me in under my real name? A little bit of a giveaway, don't you think?" He was silent far too long. Then an awkward reply, for him.

"It was a calculated risk. If anyone was watching, then it would bring them out into the open and you could eliminate them." Wow! That was not what I expected. Who does he think I am?

"I am not my mother...I am not *Olga*! I have never liked what we did and didn't really want to be involved, but as she was my only family, I didn't have a lot of choice. I grew up with all this assassination stuff as if it were normal. But it's not, and I don't want to be a part of it anymore."

I feel my pulse racing and I glance across to Freddie squirming to find a comfortable position. This ridiculous situation has been created by my mother's obsession and I want out. Having all this wealth at my disposal, means I can now do what I want. Anton listens to my rants and says nothing. He is probably processing it and working out how to persuade me to reconsider.

"Well? What do you think to what I've said?" I ask impatiently. The audio wave on my watch is a flatline. I stare at it wondering if Anton is going to say anymore. I don't give him the chance.

"Ok, if you have had enough, then will you please keep quiet so I can sleep, and we will look at a plan tomorrow. I'm too knackered to be bothered tonight." The red light in the corner of the watch face fades and I feel my shoulders relax as I slump onto the bed. I shuffle to the edge and peer down at Freddie snoring and drooling. Not his best look. Even so, my heart races and I stretch my neck so I can kiss his cheek.

"You are a star, Frederick Halbert; I would never have thought you could survive such an extreme night as this one. You have my heart even more," I say with so much emotion I nearly fall off the bed.

He squirms again as if he is listening. Maybe he is, and he feels the same way too. Or perhaps he is regretting ever knowing me. I've caused him so much grief it could be the end of a beautiful relationship before we've even started. I gather up the bed linen and scrunch it close to my body for comfort and stare through the window into the night.

The clouds are scurrying across the sky as a storm is brewing. I'm hoping that Blondie has fled the scene and doesn't show again. I think she would be better prepared next time and would not let me get away so easily. Then a thought races across my mind like the speedy clouds.

I wonder if she knows where Olga and Lee are? If so, would she now try to get them instead? I leap off the bed and touch my phone to alert Anton.

"Hey," I whisper. "Are Olga and Lee still at the hotel?"

"I will check for you."

He does his thing and comes back with a picture; one I didn't expect. They are there but in a room with a group of others. My eyes blink madly as I sit sharply upright. Olga and Lee are sitting on a sofa, handing some sort of documents to…

"BLONDIE…!"

24 - The Betrayal

Tears of anger and disbelief roll down my cheeks as I stare at the phone screen. My hands quiver uncontrollably, as my thoughts flash all over the place. What is *she* doing there? And what documents are they handing over to her? Surely, they are not working together. But why are they in the same room? Last time we were here, Olga was scared stiff at the sight of her. Now she is smiling and looking matey.

I ask Anton if he can get any real time video. He duly supplies me with a short burst. Lee is answering the door and letting Blondie in, with Olga coming to greet her. She shakes her hand, and they sit down together, as friendly as anything. What the hell is all this about? I feel like I've skipped into an alternative universe where enemies are friends and vice versa.

"Anton, can you get any sound on this?" I ask impatiently.

"Unfortunately, not. I hijacked the CCTV of the hotel which has no audio. This meeting occurred shortly after you rescued Frederick," he replies.

What? She went straight to Olga after trying to kill me? Has my world sunk into a cesspool of lies? When Olga taught me not to trust anyone - she meant it. I throw the phone onto the bed and bury my head in shaking hands. Does this mean they are in this together all along? I feel a scream raging to escape my chest but try and calm down not to wake up Freddie. It's no good - I reach for a pillow and let out an enraged yell. And then another, followed by another. That's better. Now I've cleared my head, I wonder if Anton can zoom in on the folder.

"Can you try and get a close-up of that folder? I want to see if it gives any clues." He edits the still and zooms in.

The pixels are so grainy that nothing really stands out. Another still frame flashes onto the screen. This time they have a picture, Olga sharing it with Blondie (*I must find out that bitch's name*). I recognised it at once. My mother's pendant necklace, the sapphire clearly shown.

"Is this what they are after? My mum's necklace?" Anton quickly replies.

"I said it held secrets which even I don't know or understand. Maybe they have discovered that it holds some vital information. You did bring it with you, didn't you?" he asks reservedly.

I don't remember packing it with the dress. I scurry over to my case and bags and rummage around every pocket. Then I pull out the dress and something reflects the moonlight. There it is. It must have got caught in the lining last time I wore it. Carefully I lay it on the bed next to me, wondering what mysteries this jewel holds.

"So, this is what all the fuss is about. How come these assassins didn't know what they were looking for?" I ask.

"It was the perfect camouflage from the usual mode of storage, it would have been easily overlooked by an organisation. Marian would have transported it with her all over the world, presumably using it for her contacts."

"So… if I can find the code for breaking into it…" Think …what it could be? Come on Maisie, it must be something you know or peculiar to my mum. "Anton. You said that my mother would have worn this each time she performed and took it whenever they went on missions. Do you have a log of those times?"

I sit on the edge of the bed waiting, wondering something. The phone screen flashes up videos of my mother at concerts and interviews where I can see the sapphire hanging gracefully from her smooth neck.

"You may have a clearer view from your computer. In your pack, you will find a foldable screen, which when connected to the phone will enhance the video and sound," he directs.

Well Anton, you think of everything. I rummage around in the pockets and pull out a tube containing a rolled-up foil. This must be the screen. Placing it flat on the table, it rolls back up again like an uncooperative scroll of paper.

"How does this thing stay flat?" I ask.

"You have to power it up and then it becomes rigid."

I attach the power cable to the phone and the screen smooths out as if an invisible iron had run over it. *Cool*. The screen flickers and now mirrors the phone with ultra-HD, so sharp I could cut my eyebrows with it.

Putting on the earpiece, I watch intently as mother sings like an angel, the camera panning around her as if on a current of hot air. Stage lights glint off the sapphire, sparkling with her bright eyes. I wipe away hot tears as my heart is lifted by her captivating performance. I can see why people thought so much of her. Never have I experienced such disabling emotion. If Blondie walked in now, I would be like jelly in her hand, giving no resistance.

The camera continues its ethereal flight across the stage and then out towards the audience. Men in tuxedos and bow ties, along with glamorous women in silk and chiffon nightgowns, are scattered in the auditorium, gazing in awe at my mother. I lie down across the bed and settle on my front. This is more relaxing than I thought; my eyelids are getting heavy.

I reach out for a can of coke that I half drank earlier on and rest my head on my arms. The fizz shoots up my nose and makes me cough. Freddie stirs and belches. How pleasant. Maybe this would be like marriage, one of us watching tv while the other sleeps off a rough night of drinking. I hope not. Certainly not one I want, at least.

The concert carries on to its crescendo, the stage swirling and changing in some sort of animated extravaganza, the other characters scurrying around like stage rats. The camera pulls backwards in a reverse zoom giving that sort of effect when you get too tired to focus on anything and your vision shrinks as if it's going down a tunnel. It sends me nearly to sleep, but then I notice it. Just in the corner of the shot, I see a glimpse of someone unexpected.

"Anton, go back a frame or two. There is something I need you to zoom in on." The video slowly retraces until I see it again. "There! *Stop!* Zoom in on the right-hand corner of the screen." He expands the screen until I see it, sharp as daylight. There in the audience is my father chatting to someone. Not just anyone...

I sharply sit back up, shaking. The more I sink into my past the greater the surprises and shock. It can't be her, *can it?* My father is sitting next to a woman that looks like a younger version of - *OLGA!!* What the hell? I tell Anton to do a recognition search on her face.

"It is confirmed that the woman sitting with your father is Olga Gabrys," he says without emotion.

Shaking my head, I cannot accept another revelation like this. Olga knew my father! They went to a concert where my mother was performing and enjoyed a night out together!! I feel the urge to get up and walk around, this is sending my mind into overdrive now. *Why was she there?* Was she getting into their lives ready to assassinate them? Was it a clever scheme to catch them unawares?

"Anton. When was this concert I'm looking at and where was it performed?"

"It was in Moscow, May 2010 at the Tchaikovsky Concert Hall. She was performing Wagner's 'Die Walkure' - a compelling opera of love, incest, grief, sacrifice and betrayal," he says efficiently. That just about sums up all that I'm going through - how appropriate. Maybe not the incest.

I look at the sapphire and wonder what secrets this jewel holds and why was Olga with my dad at this concert? She *was* known to them after all. Or was she there under another name? My dad seems to be quite relaxed and enjoying her company. That has always been her disarming skill, to dupe males and make them think they have all the power, when the exact opposite is the case. Could there be another reason? I know she said that there was a hit that she had to be very careful about - was this the one? Was she sizing them up ready for the kill? A thought rattles through my brain.

"Anton - you said they didn't know each other, my parents and Olga. But here she is, sitting next to my father. Is this an oversight? Or are you not as fool proof as you think… or your data provides?" I am getting sceptical of Anton's ability to give me reliable intel. He hesitates, again, making me doubt.

"It did not flag up anything, so I was not aware of Olga attending this concert. Maybe your father knew her in a different capacity. Or was it purely random?" Now he really is clutching at straws.

"Olga never does random. She has always been calculating, clever and ruthless. It was only her ability to make a mess afterwards that let her down, and that's what she relied upon me to do - clean up!"

Whatever the reason, it shows Olga was closer to my parents than I ever thought. If I give her enough time to explain, maybe the truth will come out. Seeing this video only gives me the shivers. Everything seems to be merging into one smouldering pit of crap.

I gaze at this mysterious jewel, willing it to reveal the hidden information that everyone is so eager to extract. Glancing across to Freddie still drooling onto the carpet, I smile. He is the only one in all of this that I can trust to be unconnected, unspoiled by all this underhand espionage. I hope his awful experience tonight doesn't push him away from me forever, making me very alone and desperate. It feels like a pivotal moment, a horrible tipping point which could send me to my freedom or … death.

25 - The Long Night

I sit by the open window gazing blankly at the traffic busily seeking out a destination, smelling the petrol fumes and trying to get some peace into my head. It's not easy. I'm tired and agitated, scared, and confused. I am so used to getting the information on a dispatch and then planning with Olga how to execute, tidy up and then move on; clear cut, no mess. This situation is a landfill site from start to finish. A wide, deep hole riddled with death traps.

It would be great to crack the code to release the information on this necklace and then I could understand what they are wanting. However, could it be a danger to me and anyone I know if it were out in the open? I rewind the concert in my mind and chew over something.

The message it projected asked for Marian Greene to submit the password. So, she was the only one who had it. What would it be? It could be a verbal command as there was nothing to press or engage with. So, what about her voice? Perhaps she used a range of sounds to trigger the code. Hmmm… only one way to find out.

"Anton. What audio have you got of Marian's singing and talking? I want to try something." He replies with a torrent of audio clips from her concerts and other recordings. Now, where to start? "Do you think that her singing range could be a key to opening the jewel?"

"That could work. The resonance of a voice opens many a digital vault." That has me thinking again. I wonder what her unique signature was. A soprano has a high range from what I know - which is not a lot.

"What would be the sort of resonance to activate a digital lock?" I ask. I am now venturing into things I have no clue about. Physics was never something I grasped easily.

"The lock would have to be fixed to a certain resonance for it to respond. Very good Maisie. Your theory could have merit. I can transmit her range, applying it to the sapphire and see what the result is. Would you like me to do that?"

"Yes. Make a start. The other thing is, what is happening with the huddle from hell at the hotel? Any movement?"

"I am checking... It seems that they have parted ways and Blondie has now disappeared along with two others. I could track her movements so that you can be alerted if she were to approach your hotel."

"Seems sensible. What is Olga and Lee doing?"

"Olga has now retired to bed and Lee has left for his own room." That's a surprise. I thought these two were an item.

Now I am wide awake I'm thinking I could surprise her and then nip this whole thing in the bud; get the truth out of her, finish her off and disappear, leaving Lee and Blonde floundering with nothing to show from their plans. I get a shiver, though, thinking this would be too easy. Olga is clever; she would not expose herself so carelessly. She also knows me and what I'm capable of. She did train me after all.

The racing clouds have collided, and it looks like we are going to get a torrential downpour. I can hear the distant rumbling of thunder and see occasional flashes in between the clouds. Storms have always fascinated me, the way they don't care about anyone, just roll in, do their thing, and then disappear. I suppose it mirrors my lifestyle, arrive; dispatch, and then evaporate into the night. I have lived like this since I can remember.

Olga's training included waking me at ridiculous hours in the night to be alert and ready for action whatever state of mind I was in. I now think she was creating a robot to act without the usual human emotion and care. To some extent she succeeded. I know I can be very disconnected with my emotions.

Since these few days have wrenched me from one chaotic thought to another, this impenetrable wall has been busted. Perhaps that is why I am all over the place. I don't know how to react or cope. I feel like I'm in freefall, being pushed over a cliff. Anyway, all this thinking is giving me a headache and I fumble in my bag for a tablet to take away the pain.

"Have you got anywhere yet Anton?" I ask carelessly, as I lose the first tablet down the basin waste pipe.

"Not yet. I have run 350 sound waves from Marian's voice and still the stone has not responded. I will keep trying." Good dog! Although he would not like being called that.

I am still puzzled why my mother would keep this information out of Anton's storage. Did she doubt he was safe? Or did she not trust his loyalty? Was it anything to do with my dad? Was he kept out of the loop as well? Questions, questions I torment myself with. I reach for another pill.

"Do you think I would be safe to go for a walk - my mind is overheating and it's getting stuffy in here," I ask Anton. Why, I am not sure, as I don't need his permission. I am treating him like Olga now.

"You can obviously do as you please. However, ensure that Frederick is secure, and the room is tamper-proof. I will continue with my work." The red-light flickers and dies. Well, at least he didn't tell me to keep a low profile.

I gather my waterproofs and look at the range of weapons I perhaps should take - just in case. With the weather likely to be wet, a taser isn't a good idea, so I attach my cord with its knife to my leg and console myself that my fighting skills are probably adequate for a Parisian Street fight. Why I am expecting a fight, I'm not sure, but perhaps I'm so fired up because of all these revelations. The suit that saved me earlier is still in the bath soaking so that's no use. I'll be fine, what am I worried about? It couldn't get any worse than what just happened to me, surely?

Making sure that Freddie is going to be out of it, I dress and quietly exit the room. The rest of the hotel seems still and eerily dead. No one in the corridors, no one in the foyer, only the receptionist who appears to be nodding off. All the lights in the lounges and downstairs rooms are dimmed or off, making for a half-light dreaminess.

Zipping up my coat, the cooler air hits my face as I step outside onto the sidewalk. The smell of fumes has been replaced with a sweeter, aromatic smell that comes from stormy weather. I read somewhere that the ozone in the air changes when lightning strikes, creating this unworldly scent. Whatever it is, I welcome it and scrunch up my coat around my neck and stride out along the street towards my favourite place in Paris - The Louvre.

It's bringing a lightness to my steps as I skip alongside the River Seine, a sense of freedom from everything that has been dumped on me. I'm still a bit edgy though when the occasional person walks by. My heart flutters and my eyes are crisscrossing scanning to make sure they are not interested in me, but after the tenth time of doing that, I relax and just enjoy the solitude.

The clouds are lit up by the street lighting and the Eiffel Tower pushing upwards towards the stars, which remain hidden. The rumble of thunder is echoing around the city, bouncing off the buildings sounding like a crash of dumpsters. A streak of lightning ripples through the sky. It briefly illuminates the clouds with a purple and red lattice violently grasping hold of empty air.

My mind is on a video loop, musing over what the future holds. I'm trying not to get too depressed about it. That must wait because of all the other crap that needs to be sorted before. Yet, it still weighs on me like a ton of rocks. I hate it when you are awake at night and your mind goes on overdrive, making you think that you are a lunatic and life is ending before daybreak. Perhaps it could be this time, the way my life is heading. *NO, Maisie*! Stop this rubbish! It will work out ok. I have a plan, of sorts, and Olga will give me the truth and she will pay for what she did!

Another flash startles me, followed by a low rumble and then - *bloody hell*! A crash so loud it shakes the ground. The lightning reflects off the river giving a spectacular mirror image, making me stop and stare into empty space. A drunken man staggers along the waterfront, singing some French song, briefly stopping to look at me. He waves as if I know him. I wave back. He shouts something with a very loud garbled voice and then trips over himself, the bottle of his demise rolling off into the water.

"*Merde*," he grumbles, and pulls another one out from his jacket and continues with his song. His comical actions cause me to laugh. Alcohol though, is such a destroyer of people, greater than what Olga and I have done over the years. At least he seems happy in his own world. Or perhaps he is just masking the pain from something and it's his way of coping.

I'm not sure how *I* am coping, and I breathe in deeper to clear my head. I switch on my playlist and Ed Sheeran warbles out "Stop the Rain"; quite apt I think, as it begins to pour. I run across quickly to the Louvre complex of fountains and the famous glass pyramid.

It brings back soft memories of Freddie and me dashing around through the water laughing and splashing each other. It was this first meeting that captured my heart, and I have so longed to see him again. This crazy situation we find ourselves in just annoys me so much. I am frightened that he will ghost me and then I will lose any chance of normality. The rain creates a blanket to all the views I love, so I try and get some cover under a balcony. I wipe my face and blink out the water, my hair now flapping wildly, wrapping itself around my face as the wind has gone crazy.

I stare out through a waterfall cascading from a broken downpipe across to the glass pyramid which is hazy through the rain. All that were out for a late-night walk seem to have disappeared like me, diving for cover. The wind whistling and the rain lashing down is all I hear, not the peaceful walk I was hoping for. At least it should be refreshing in a way, and maybe give me some reason to sleep. Another flash of lightning illuminates the courtyard area, followed by thunder which rattles the stonework. Phew, I am expecting a strike any minute the way this is going on.

I'm distracted by movement diagonally from where I am sheltering and makes my heart flutter. *Was that…?* Another flash lights up the whole area as bright as day for a second. A person is moving around in a weird way, and I fixate on their route. I am not sure who I saw, perhaps I'm imagining, but I thought it looked like - *Lee*!

I feel my hands tense up, my reaction to any threat. I can't seem to control it; it must be a reflex after all the years of training. I stare at the figure weaving around the fountains. Are they coming towards me or trying to avoid someone else? I quickly scan around to see if any other person is tracing them. Over the far end of the complex, I can see a group, maybe two or three tracking the person's movements. So, at least it's not me he's after.

I can see that the group are carrying some sort of weapon. Keeping their weapons high, their body posture indicates they are preparing to attack. I switch my attention to Lee who now is ducking and keeping himself low. Does he really think he's not obvious? It's almost comical watching this. I cross my arms and lean against the stonework hoping whoever is chasing catches him and gives me one less job to do.

Suddenly, a crack of lightning flashes across the water and hits something on a building sending sparks cascading everywhere. It shocks me and I fall to the ground, doing my Black Widow stance, ready for anything. I see the person caught like a deer in a car's headlights staring straight towards me. *It is Lee!*

He gazes across to where I am for a second in the afterglow of the blast and then runs off towards the river. The chasers pick up pace now and run at full pelt aiming their tactical weapons. They remind me of the French balaclava brigade in that service station. They run faster now, closing in on him. I find myself willing them on. *Come on you can do it.*

Another lightning flash reflects off the glass pyramid like a mirror ball at a disco, sending shafts of light in all directions. I see Lee turn and check where his chasers are; he ducks and draws a handgun. This should be interesting, Lee against a small battalion with semi-automatics.

They come closer and I can see that they *are* dressed like the service station attackers, black skin suits and body armour. For whatever reason they resist firing even though they are so close now they could blast him to bits. They bore down on him and slow their advance. I hear them shouting something, but the wind is carrying the words away. Lee is shouting back in French, I think. Wow - he is cultured after all.

They halt and point their weapons uncompromisingly. There is no way Lee is getting out of this alive. A lot of shouting and chatting seems to follow, which irritates my sense of urgency. *For God's sake, dispatch Lee and get off!* I am resisting the urge to run over and snatch one of the weapons and do the job myself.

This standoff seems to last far too long, with Lee now standing upright, lowering his weapon. The group also lower their semi-automatics, as if a parle is going on. What are they talking about? The wind is whistling and distorting any sound coming from them, and I'm resisting trying to get closer.

Then, as abruptly as it all started, the group ran off in the other direction from where Lee was dashing to. Very peculiar. I watch carefully as the group disappear down a side street whilst keeping my eyes on Lee's escape route. He seems to be tracing back along where I have just been. He obviously didn't see me in that flash of lightning, or he would have come towards me.

Double checking the others have left, I venture out from my hideaway and follow Lee a few hundred meters behind. I don't want to get him all excited at finding me and then the game will be over, one way or another. He continues along the Seine scanning about making sure no one is following him, I guess. We pass the drunk who is now cursing the weather and looking less happy.

Still the wind and rain lashes down, making it difficult to keep a visual on him. He moves a mobile to his ear and briefly stops to talk, then walks more urgently, breaking into a jog. I am wondering if this is Olga or someone else chatting to him. Could it be that Lee is double crossing Olga? My conspiracy theories are running wild in my head at this point. He heads across one of the bridges that takes you on to the island where Notre Dame sits. Perhaps he's friends with Quasimodo?

The rain eases a little, along with less thunderclaps, as I follow him along the Quai de la Corse. Is he heading for the hospital? It would appear not as he continues past there. I trace his steps and watch as he enters the Notre Dame complex, still cordoned off due to its restoration.

He slips through a gate and disappears, so I quicken my pace. I don't want to lose him now. I'm curious as to what he's up to. Maybe I'm having feelings of protectiveness towards Olga. Damn, I hope not. But this is too intriguing, and I am compelled to follow.

I carefully squeeze through the gate, making a creaking noise. I grasp it, glancing around. Hopefully no one heard that, so I carry on tiptoeing around some work cabins. I hear Lee's voice inside. I shuffle up below one of the windows and press against the cold metal. This is when I could do with my amazing glasses which would allow me to listen in and see through the walls.

He is chatting to someone in there. I hear another person answering. It's all in French, and mine is so rubbish I can't understand any of it. I do pick out my name though, my spine tingling with anger. Another word *'Saphir'* which I guess is the jewel. So, they are talking about me and that bloody sapphire. But who is he talking to? I am incensed about this, and I must get a visual on the other person. Climbing onto a concrete plinth, I edge up to the window. *Blast!* I slip as everything is so wet and my hand bangs on the metal. *Shit*!

I make a dash for another cabin and slip out of sight. I hear Lee opening a groaning door, the other person sounding alarmed. Crunching footsteps echo in between the cabins as someone is searching for the noise maker. My heart is racing, and my hands are tensing. I've got to be quick and decisive if he finds me. The footsteps stop, the fine drizzle being the only noise. The wind has died down too, making me hypersensitive to any other sounds. There's an owl hooting from some high up buttress and a distant police siren penetrating the silence. I can even hear Lee's breathing.

To my relief, the crunching starts again and returns to the cabin, a door clanging closed. I peek out and scan the area around me, confirming no one is outside. I'm spooked now, so I slip back through the gate. I decide to take up a more remote position and watch for any activity. I didn't come with any kit that would have made this easier, so I must sit and wait old-style, using my eyes and ears.

The cold night air is beginning to make this uncomfortable as my butt is cold and wet on the stonework. I move without giving too much away, shuffling side to side trying to get my blood moving. Why did I think coming out was a good idea? The warm hotel room is clawing at my cold skin. Just a few more moments, that's all it will take - *come on Maisie, you're getting weak.*

A crack of light darts across the yard. The door opens slowly, a torrent of French exchanges and Lee walks out throwing his hands around in a typical European style. Is the meeting over with? He walks away looking back once and swears. It's funny; everyone seems to know when someone swears in whatever language, more to do with body expression than words.

Keeping an eye on the open door, I am willing whoever is in there to come out so I can ID them or at least get Anton to. A shadow blots out the light and for a moment I see the silhouette of a tall, elegantly dressed man standing on the threshold. The interior light goes off, replaced by torchlight. I couldn't make out the face and trying to get a picture in this light on my phone was not even worth it.

Lee continues towards the gate and scuttles off towards his hotel. The man saunters down to the gate and stops as if he has smelt something. I push myself further back into the stonework. Can he sense me? My heart races again and my breath is pouring out clouds of steam like a train. He scans around, his eyes like beacons searching for a movement. Then, after a pause which seemed like a year, he moves off and I hear the squawk of a car alarm and the rev of an engine. At the squeal of tyres, I reappear and blink to get my eyes at maximum strength. Hmmm… a British number plate. At least I can give Anton *something*.

The walk back to the hotel gets my mind buzzing with these two weird episodes. Lee was acting independent of Olga. So, was it agreed or is he involved in something else? All this seems unimportant as the waterproof I'm wearing is soaked and obviously not giving me any protection from this rubbish weather. I start to run just to get warm again. I hear the drunk singing even louder now; I hope he doesn't end up in the river!

The approach to my hotel gives my heart a jump as I'm going back to Freddie and I'm wondering how and what to tell him about me. My whole life has become so complicated, it seems like a fantasy. I just hope he wakes up less aggravated so I can explain. The swing doors open with a swish and the receptionist is still wavering between this world and dream land. I am far from sleepy though, so I ask her if the hotel gym is open.

"Oui, mademoiselle. Here is the key. You should be quite alone at this time of night," she replies.

That is fine by me. I usually work out at silly times when no one is awake. I crash into the weights area and strip down to my underwear. I should be ok - no old guys will be perving over me at this time. I choose the running machine to set me off, then the rowing machine and some simple weights on the multi gym.

The adrenaline hits me after 30 minutes of full throttle and then I wind down drinking as much water as my gut will allow. Back to the walker and then into the shower. It has been a long night but now at last I feel energised and tired enough at the same time to sleep for a couple of hours. Tomorrow will be the day to get busy and bring all this to a satisfying end - *I hope.*

I creep back into my room expecting Freddie to be in my bed and looking all ready for action, but sadly he is still sprawled out on the floor looking less desirable than before. I sling a blanket over him and tuck a cushion under his head, careful not to catch his congealed cuts. Slinking into bed, I turn the light off allowing the street lighting to cast an amber glow through the window and I drift off finally thinking about nothing.

26 - *The Kiss and Tell*

My watch alarm is the first thing I hear at 6.30am and nearly crap myself when Freddie is not on the carpet in front of the bed. I frantically search the room for him. Has he sneaked out and disappeared? Then I hear the toilet flush and so sink back into the pillows relieved. He crashes through the door staring at me.

"What? Are you ok?" I ask quietly. He has freshened up and no longer has the look of a beaten-up cage fighter, although his clothes are smudged with stains.

"Hmmm.... you care about such things, Maisie? If that's your real name." He gives me a suspicious glance and sits on the edge of the bed. I nod.

"Of course, I do, and it is... silly arse." I look away knowing I must give some sort of justification that doesn't sound ridiculous. "I have a lot to explain and it's difficult for me to tell you as I don't want you to freak out." I look sheepishly at his dark brown eyes, giving me that '*try me*' look.

"Well... *I am* Maisie, but not Maisie Gabrys, as I thought. I am apparently Maisie Greene, daughter of British parents who are now dead. Olga adopted me when I was young. It's all new to me too Freddie, and I've had a hell of a couple of days of being shot at and chased all over the place. And then you got involved in it and... *I'm so sorry,*" I blurt out, like a crazed idiot.

Staring into his eyes, I see they are still reflecting mistrust. I keep checking myself as to how much to give away, as it might put him in further danger. We have a moment's silence. He raises a hand as if to point at something.

"Ok... I get that. You know I am adopted and finding out about your biological parents is harsh. I only recently found out about mine. I asked Maman to get the records and it was hard to find out they were dead. But... What about all the shooting... and me getting snatched by this psycho woman? She was asking strange questions about you which I did not understand. That is weirder," he says with hurt. I nod again and move a little closer.

"I know... I am so angry that it happened this way. What did she say about me?" I ask, my heart fluttering like a moth caught in a net.

"She said you were hiding something that she wanted. It was hers and you had stolen it. You were involved in things that were pissing off her employer and she was determined to get it back and wasn't going to stop at nothing." He flinched as he said this. "She kept on hitting me as if I knew something and I kept on saying that I didn't. So, what was it she wanted? I think I deserve to know why I went through all that," he said trailing off as he got up to walk around.

"Yeah...you do. But to be honest I'm not sure what it is either. I can only think it's some information that is very important to someone," I say, pursing my lips. This is so close to telling him too much and I'm scared that it will send him away from me forever. "Look…. Olga is not what I thought she was, and I am trying to track her down as I need to get the truth out of her. Then, I'm sure this thing that Blondie is after will make itself clear." He stares at me again.

"Why is Olga not with you? You have fallen out?"

"Yeah, you could say that."

"So… she is here in Paris, can we sort this out quickly and then get this crazy blonde out of your life?" He makes it sound like a family reunion will patch things over.

"Not that easy I'm afraid...I have to do some crazy shit to get this sorted. Things that you wouldn't want to know," I say as he frowns and paces up and down.

"Did you contact me to help you with this?"

"No… I really wanted to see you and have some fun, honestly."

"Hmmm... not much fun so far," he says, a slight grin creasing his face.

"Nope... not the romantic time I was looking forward to." He stops and his eyes widened. Was that too much information? I feel my face flush.

He takes a step towards me and then hesitates. He holds out a hand. I respond and get off the bed and reach for him. My heart is racing more than when I am under attack from a rain of bullets. A rush of heat races up my back and makes me blink. He pulls me closer, and I feel his strong-arm wrap around my waist. My first instinct is to twist his arm and throw him over my shoulder as I've done with most males, I've got this close to, but resist the urge.

He looks down at me with a smile and I feel my face relax and I giggle like a five-year-old girl. What are these feelings? I feel like jelly. He wraps his other arm around my neck and pulls me close. The heat of his body brings a feeling of security and I squeeze my arms around his waist, accidentally brushing across the top of his butt cheeks. It sends the strangest pleasure through my head as we look at each other and gently kiss on soft lips.

"*Ow*," he yells and jerks back. I forgot his lips were cracked from the beating. I gently touch them with my fingers and kiss him on the cheek. He responds by moving his hands down to my hips. I am now overwhelmed with a passion alien to me. My hands wander down his back to his butt cheeks again and squeeze as if I'm kneading bread. He shivers as I sense he wants me too. This is not quite what I expected from our second time together. Maybe all the shit we have been through is forcing us closer and quicker than either of us thought. Then...the thing I could do without - at this moment of lust and *amour*.

"Maisie...I have some updated information," Anton briskly chirps out, frightening Freddie so much he staggers back looking like he was expecting to see his mother sitting on the couch watching us. Bloody hell, what a time for an update!

"Oh God, Anton! Why do you have to spoil everything?" I say, so annoyed I could throw the phone out of the window. I breathe in deeply and raise a hand to Freddie. "It's ok... it's only a computer that is helping me find Olga and with everything else that is going on... *bloody hell* Anton... your timing is ... *argh*!" Freddie sits down as if I've told him the worst news ever.

"It is imperative that you act quickly as Olga and Lee are leaving the hotel and have secured a car, destination unknown," he says urgently. Oh great, now I must revert to my insane assassin nature again.

"Ok... where can I get a car from at short notice?" I ask.

"That would be difficult as you are underage and have no licence to drive in France," Anton cheerfully says.

"That's not helpful Anton."

Freddie shakes his head. "You are talking to a computer? *Merde*. This is getting stranger all the time!" he says, shaking his head.

"Yeah, I know it is weird and once this is sorted, I'm kicking him into touch. Anton, I need to get something to follow them. What can I do?" I ask impatiently. The frustration builds in me. I cannot let Olga and Lee disappear now. Freddie looks across at me and holds out both hands.

"I could get one of my father's cars and we could follow in that, if that helps" he says. I gawp at him and close my mouth and then ask if that is a real offer.

"Yes of course. He has a great selection of vehicles as a diplomat." I nod vigorously and run over to him, kissing him too hard on his lips. He recoils again.

"Sorry!"

A thrill runs up my back as I am so excited; we are finally going to chase them down. "Great. Come on, we must get ready to leave. How much time Anton before they get their hired car?"

"Thirty minutes."

"Ok. Can we get one of your dads and then track them?" I ask Freddie.

"Oui, it should be possible. But where are we going? I have to give some explanation."

"Hmmm... yes that will be difficult as we have no idea where they are going," I say, shrugging and then stuffing all my clothes and kit into my bags. It's a good job I showered after my gym session, or I would be stinking Freddie out of the car.

"We will have to give some lame excuses, I'm afraid. You are taking me on a sightseeing tour of Paris ... or France, or something. Come on, you can do it," I say, trying to encourage him to move.

"Ok. We can do that. But I will have to change. I cannot be seen out in this mess," he says with a grimace. I smile and nod knowing how proud he is of his style even if it is a bit off the wall.

Making sure that all my kit and the sapphire is stashed away, and my suit is now dry and recharged, we dash off throwing the keys in at reception and wave down a cab, Freddie giving the directions to where his parents keep their vehicles.

We hold hands in the back seat, almost making it feel like a normal day out. The cab races via the Arc De Triomphe into the Neurilly-sur-Seine area where we will hopefully get some transport. I squeeze Freddie's hand and mouth thank you. He smiles back and flicks his hair over to one side showing his tattoo visible under the shaved side of his head. A fleur-de-lis along with a rooster sit side by side. I hadn't noticed that before.

"Your tattoos - when did you get them? They're so cool," I ask casually. He shrugs.

"About two years ago. I was the lead guitarist in a band called the 'Le Fleur du Coq', so I thought it a good idea to mash two symbols of French history," he says with a smug nod. I laugh.

"The Flower of the Cock?" I say, bursting with laughter again.

"The Flower of the Cockrell, you funny woman," he replies, shaking his head. "A symbol of French dignity and resistance."

"I thought it was used as a symbol for troublemakers in the French revolution," I reply, biting my lip. "Quite appropriate for you, I think." He glances at me rolling his eyes.

We pull each other closer as his arm loops around my neck, the taxi winding its way along busier streets. Being with him is surreal, especially as he is now helping me in my day job.

"We did gigs all over Paris. The night clubs and bars would have us for a couple of nights. Some of the band were idiots though and eventually we stopped as the police were constantly on our case for disrupting these places," he continues, smirking over his rebellious past. "It was my father that told me not to carry on as it would reflect badly on the family and his work. So, I thought it was a good idea to pull out." He glances at me and smiles, sending a shiver down my spine. His dark skin and almost black eyes drag me in. I kiss his cheek again.

"Hey. You are a little forward for a second date, non?" he says, turning to face me. I grin back and for a moment I think that I am more like Olga than I thought.

Her seductive ways must have rubbed off onto me. I am not afraid of this encounter, but wary of my feelings. Also, I'm not sure how much you are supposed to let your guard down with a boy you have only known for a short time. The swerving taxi though, doesn't give me any more time to think it through as we arrive at Freddie's house. We scramble out of the car and stand in front of huge iron gates. He buzzes the intercom and confirms who he is.

"Sorry Maisie, you will have to wait here as I am the only one who can enter the compound," he says apologetically. I shrug and sit down on the low wall.

"I'll wait here then – oh and get something to eat for breakfast. I don't know how long this will take, so better be prepared." He looks oddly at me. "And... make sure we have some coke; I run on the stuff, I'm afraid. And no booze for you!" He nods and laughs.

"You will not keep that gorgeous waistline if you keep drinking shit like that," he says, as a buzzer opens the gate. He disappears behind some hedging, and I gather my bags together at my feet. At least it's not raining now, and the fresh damp air has lightened the stuffy atmosphere.

I feel my nerves jangling as I consider what I am about to do. The thought of killing Olga hasn't really sunk in too much. But I can't do that with Freddie around, so this car chase will have to be for recon at most. I glance at the time, my leg bouncing up and down. I hope he's not going to take forever, as this whole trip will be a wasted opportunity.

Watching people walking about their daily lives, I blow my cheeks out and sigh. If I could be like them one day, that would be my dream. No pressure to dispatch anyone, just get up, wander the streets and shop. No expectations to defend myself or clean up Olga's mess. Bliss.

My eyes follow a girl walking a dog and smile. It's a cockapoo, fawn in colour and as lively as a horse. The girl is laughing and trying to keep it under control. I've never had a pet, as we moved around so much it would be another inconvenience. She comes closer and the dog bounces over to me, tongue hanging out. I reach over and rub its ears. The girl begins to ramble on about something and I look as interested as I can and nod, throwing my hands out, thinking that gesture was typically French, hoping that would satisfy her. Except, she just looks puzzled as I do to her, and then speaks English.

"You are a funny person - you live around here? I am from the French Embassy. You know Monsieur Halbert? He lives here, non?" I nod and say I am waiting for Frederick. Her face brightens up at his name.

"*Frederick* - I like him lots. He is super cool. I have some of his music. I think he is crazy too," she says with wild excitement. Obviously, she has a crush on him.

"Hey... I think I might have some competition! You never know, he might sign your arm when he comes out," I say as a whisper. She giggles like I did this morning.

"Really? That would be amazing." I nod and pat the dog again and try to redirect its cocking leg.

At that moment my eyes catch the sight of someone in slow motion, walking on the opposite side. Instinctively, I flip my hood up and lower my gaze. Fortunately, there are enough trees down this street to shield me from view. I thought it looked like the man from last night's encounter with Lee. Same suit, walk and posture. Where is he going? The girl starts up another chat but now I'm distracted. I must resist tracking him as we cannot miss the chance of chasing Olga and Lee, but I am so torn. Come on Freddie, where is that damn car?

"You like him too?" the girl insists. I nod and smile.

"Yes, I do. Do you know a lot of people around here?" I ask, changing the subject.

"Oui, I have lived here all my life."

"So, would you know who that is, over there?" She follows my gaze.

"Arr, oui; he is British, I think. I don't know his name, but he is here a lot."

"Oh wow, thank you. And what's your name?"

"Nicolette," she answers brightly. "Et vous?"

"Erm… Maisie." She studies my face as if she sees a blackhead.

"Oh, that is a great name, after the singer." I frown and say maybe.

"You have a lovely name too," I say, now looking anxiously at my watch.

Freddie's probably having a sauna at this rate. I stand up and watch the man skip up the steps into an official building. The dog is looking as restless as I feel, and then I hear a roaring sound from behind the gates. Nicolette and I stand back as they open and a bright orange bonnet sneaks out. What the hell has he got to drive? We both stand in awe as this sports car gently pulls across the sidewalk.

"My God! It's a McLaren 600lt!" I spit out, nearly choking. I run my fingers over the bonnet as the door silently lifts. "A 3.8ltr V8 with 7 speed shift!" I duck down and stare at Freddie who is beaming.

"Wow, you know your cars, Maisie Greene!" he says looking impressed. "Come on; we had better be going as they will be gone forever." I stop my gawking and say goodbye to the girl and dog, throwing my bags on top of him. Nicolette waves madly at the sight of Freddie, (*not the car*) and mimes him signing her arm.

"You have another fan," I say, smiling at him. "She has your music and wants her arm to be signed. Is that ok?" I nuzzle up to him.

"Of course, but we must go, yes?" I nod and shout out that Freddie will sign it when he comes back. The door closes and the engine revs as I fit into the bucket seats as if we are on a space mission.

"You could have chosen a less obtrusive car. It's a bit bright for following someone," I say, giving him a scowl. He frowns, shoving the bags back to me and hesitates.

"Well… I wanted to impress you, that is all," he says as his face glows a little darker.

"Are you blushing? *Ha* … I *am* impressed. Come on, let's go. You can impress me more when this is all over." I wink at him, making him splutter, much to my satisfaction.

27 - The Car Chase

He revs out of the gateway and down the street towards the Arc de Triomphe taking it slower than I would like. His gear changing seems a little erratic. Has he driven this before?

"Are you ok driving?" He nods and scrambles the gears again.

"It has been a while since I drove this car. I will get used to it in a moment," he smiles.

"Ok. But we have only 5 minutes before they get their hire car." I look down at the time on the dash and need Anton to give an update.

"Anton. Where are Olga and Lee? I hope they are still in the hotel." The pause sends panic through me.

"Yes. They have established themselves in the foyer waiting for the car to arrive. I have been tracking Blondie also. I have discovered her name. Would you like to know?"

"Yes, I do!" Freddie glances at me, narrowly missing a pedestrian. "Please concentrate, as I'm beginning to wonder if I should drive," I snap, as he has no idea of my driving experience and is making me nervous. So, Blondie has a name. I can feel my heart racing at the thought.

"She is of South African background, called Harmony Chase. She has had connections with MI6 in the past before contracting out to the agency and other organisations. As I have said, her present affiliations are unknown."

"Thank you, Anton. I don't know whether knowing her name helps me or not. But at least the MI6 info is interesting." I try to join the dots that are appearing in front of my eyes. Perhaps I need a coke.

"Yes, could my parents have had some prior contact?" At this, Freddie screws up his face and gives me a worried look.

"What is all this talk of MI6 and agencies? Are you some sort of spy?" His face seems to lose colour.

"Just keep driving and don't think too much. Let's focus on getting Olga in sight and following. No big deal, Ok?" I say as firmly as I dare, as he could bail out at any minute if he gets any more jitters.

"Let *me* talk to Anton and *you* get us to the hotel. Now, Anton, where do you think the connection is here? I saw a guy meeting Lee last night who's a British diplomat, supposedly, based here in Paris. Also, Lee had a face to face with a trained group of elite soldiers who were tracking him and then weirdly had a chat and dispersed. What could that be about?"

"There would appear to be a coalition of interests at play. You say a group of elite soldiers?"

"Yes, black suits, semi-automatic weapons, night vision."

"That description could point to the DGSE, an elite black ops unit. The French must be after the information the stone holds." I notice that Freddie is looking more anxious as sweat is pouring down his face.

"Are you ok Freddie? Do we need the air-con higher?" I ask. He shakes his head and sprays me. *"Oi! Thanks!* Why are you looking so worried? I know all this is a bit weird…"

He puts his hand up. "Do not get involved with these people Maisie - you don't understand what they can do."

"Why? Have you heard of them?" I ask, wondering what he's on about. He hesitates as we pass the hotel where Olga and Lee should be waiting and pulls up a hundred meters away. He turns to me, a quiver in the corner of his mouth, waving his hand.

"They are France's finest, most ruthless soldiers. I should know - my father trained as one!" I feel a deep pit form in my stomach. Not one that makes me wretch, but a feeling of repulsion. I can feel myself backing away from him. His father is one of these assassins?

"I can see that this makes you worried, but I am more worried Maisie. My father is now a diplomat but still has connections with this special-ops command." He looks even more agitated as he wrings his hands on the steering wheel.

"Does this mean I have brought you into a scrap between the British and French? The rabbit hole gets deeper," I say, trying not to let my mistrust grow.

I am distracted by movement at the front of the hotel. A car pulls up and Olga and Lee appear with their bags and suitcases. Pulling myself into a professional mindset, I flick Freddie with the back of my hand to get him to concentrate on following.

"Ok...come on. We will have to assume he knows nothing about me or what is going on, or he wouldn't have let you have the car, surely. Let's focus on this and when it's all over, we can chill."

I am not sure that was very persuasive as he nods vigorously and continues to sweat like Niagara Falls. Olga's car pulls away and I wave my hand to get Freddie to move as well. He responds by nearly stalling but recovers without shooting too much grey smoke out the back, revving like a joy rider.

"Cool it, Freddie. Keep a good 100 meters behind and we will not be noticed - I hope." He nods again and calms his jerky driving.

We move off, the streets becoming almost grid locked. At this distance we should be ok, as the traffic is crawling at a walking frame pace. I search Freddie's face for any more clues to what he just told me. My lifetime of mistrust is gnawing at me, telling me not to have confidence in him, but I'm resisting it. He is *not* the one I can push away.

"Please tell me more about this French op group. How long was he with them?" I ask.

"Hmm… about 5 years. It was when I was younger, and we moved around France from place to place as his work demanded. Only when I was in my teens did he settle here in Paris and then became a diplomat. My mother and I found life settled down at last and we had a home." I stare ahead.

"Yeah… tell me about it. I don't think I can call anywhere home. Except maybe the place I've just come across. It's really nice in the middle of the countryside and a small village and…" I think about my grandmother and stop talking.

"Oh, sounds idyllic. What is this place?" I look at him as I hold back a tear.

"Somewhere I *could* call home, that's all," I say and turn back to staring through the windscreen. "Is that their car, turning right? Yes, it is. Make sure you don't lose them through the lights," I urge Freddie. He scrambles the gears again and revs so high the tyres squeal, sending us spinning sideways.

"*Watch it!* We are *trying* to keep a low profile," I say, grimacing at the choice of my words.

"Oui, oui I am nearly shitting myself but don't worry, we will keep following," he gasps, weaving through stationary traffic. The lights are on red. I glance both ways expecting a crash but amazingly we whizz effortlessly around the corner, as I hear a mash up of vehicles behind us.

"Well done, that was a neat move," I say, sounding slightly patronizing. He smiles as a look of confidence appears on his face.

"I am getting used to this car at last," he says, looking pleased with himself.

I pat him on the leg and then squeeze it. He glances at me and looks even more pleased. We are now beside the river heading towards the Eiffel Tower. Passing Notre Dame reminds me of the meeting of Lee with this mysterious man and gets me wondering.

"Your dad; did he ever work with MI6 do you know? Or another agency?" I ask, searching for any clues. Freddie glances around as if someone might be listening.

"Is your computer hearing this?" he asks.

"No… I have turned it off. He is only on when the red light shows… here on my watch or phone." I show him. He becomes agitated again.

"I remember a time when he was talking to Maman about an agency that the French authorities were tracking down. He never said who they were, but he was angry about it." I feel myself gulp and wonder if this is the same one Olga (and me) worked for.

"Do you know anything else from that conversation? It might just help us," I ask hopefully. He shakes his head.

"They rarely said anything about his work then, or even now." We pass the tower and I crane my neck to look up at this iron monster. "It took him away often, to other countries, always secretive operations. I asked him once about them, and he was quick to tell me not to ask again. It would not be safe for me to know anything." I nod, understanding *that*.

"I found some documents though, and because I was not supposed to look… of course, *I did*! They were full of chemical signs and written in many languages. The one that was in French I read quickly, and it was shocking," he says, looking a little paler.

"Oh… sounds intriguing. What did it say?"

"Some organization was producing a genetically enhanced airborne deterrent. You English would call a 'dirty bomb'." He stares, fixed like a hare gazing into truck headlights. Oof, I'm not liking the sound of *that*. We are turning away from the river now and heading out of Paris. I see a sign D910 and Versailles. Could that be their destination?

"Anything else? Where or who?" I ask, trying to get a grip of what his dad was into.

"Non. There were pictures of people and maps which I didn't have time to look at as Papa was about to find me and I ran out of the room. Maisie, it was scary stuff. I hope you are not into anything like that." I give a flat smile trying to give nothing away.

We are travelling faster now as I watch Olga's car weaving in and out of the traffic ahead. I wonder what Freddie's dad would think of his son dating the daughter of an agency assassin. Probably wouldn't go down too well as he would be choking on his morning croissant at this very moment, especially when I am being driven in his elite sports car. I muse over the weird coincidence that Freddie and I have something in common, even though he doesn't realise.

I press back into the seat that wraps around my back and rear as if it's a comfy friend. I rest my head and turn to Freddie who is now relaxing more and enjoying his chance to drive such a great car. His style of clothes is a bit retro, with a jacket that looks like it came out of the nineties and black leather trousers, along with black laced up boots. His maroon shirt hides underneath, the collar teasing itself out from around his neck. From there a chain hung, made of what, I do not know. His ears are studded with swords and crosses, with a small tattoo at the base of his right ear. All very weird for a child of the 2000's, but I like it. I wander a hand over to his leg and rub it up and down. He makes a silly squealing noise.

"Be careful - I don't want to crash!" he says with a smile and places his hand on mine. He glances in the rear mirror and before he can say anything, I feel pressed back in the seat. The car is suddenly speeding up.

"What's wrong? Why are you going faster?" I quiz. His face is set on the road and I'm anxiously looking around. "Is there someone following us?" He nods and weaves through the busy lanes. "Who have you seen?"

"It is a black van with diplomatic plates. I sometimes saw them when Papa was with the DGSE. It came out of nowhere, speeding up to us." He bites his top lip and wipes his brow.

I am feeling sweaty too. Could it be the same clowns that attacked us in Britain, the same as Lee met last night? This is getting too obvious. How do they know we are here?

"Are you sure they are chasing us? Maybe they are going somewhere else, on a training mission or something?" I say, trying to be logical about it, but I can't help feeling twitchy. Freddie shakes his head. I can see fear building in his eyes.

"Keep calm Freddie. Don't act crazy or that will bring more attention to us," I tell him. I glance back and try to make out who is in the van. The blacked-out windows only reflect the morning sun, so that's no use. I flick on my phone.

"Anton. We are being followed by a DGSE troop van. Can you get any intel on this for us?"

"Of course. I am switching to their feed. I shall monitor any chatter and will inform you as soon as I can," he chirps away.

"Your computer can hack into their systems? Is this thing legal?" Freddie asks, groaning.

"Oui monsieur, it is legal if you are a spy," I say, sarcastically. He gives me a sharp sidewards look.

"You *are* a spy then?"

"*Non, non*...I get rid of spies when they turn rogue." Oops... that was silly. Now I must back track if I'm going to keep his confidence. "*What* do you think I am, Freddie boy?" Perhaps asking this question is not going to give me or him any reassurance.

"That remains to be seen, I guess, Maisie Greene," he says reservedly.

I smile and blow him a kiss. He swerves around a tanker lorry and being so low down, I can see through to the other side. I instinctively sink further down in the seat as I spot Olga and Lee parallel with us.

"Shit! You've overtaken them! They are just over there. I think you need to slow down." Freddie doesn't look convinced. I look in the side mirror and can see the van is keeping up with us. Anton butts in.

"I have found the van but there seems to be no chatter on the DGSE comms. They would seem to be independent," he says.

"Meaning…?" I ask.

"They are possibly acting without the usual sanction of the French Military. Maybe, this is the reason behind the clandestine meeting with Lee and them. I can only guess." Freddie gives me another odd look. I smile sweetly back.

As we pass the tanker I search around for Olga's car. We have merged onto another road now which leads to Versailles. It must be where they are going. In all the speeding up and slowing down they have got in front of us again, so I direct Freddie to keep them in sight and stop worrying about this van.

"OK. We are going to have to play this carefully. There is no reason to act crazy because of these people driving the same way as we are. Perhaps it's a coincidence - maybe not. At least we are prepared," I say with authority from my experience. Freddie nods and points to the signs. Olga *is* heading for Versailles.

"That confirms where we are going then. I wonder what she and Lee are doing there?" I ask.

"Maybe they are just sightseeing - not that unusual really. Only *you* are unusual Maisie," he says with a half-smile. I laugh and reach across and kiss his cheek. Anton comes to life again.

"I have received a message from MI6 regarding the 'dirty bomb'. I have grave news for you, I'm afraid. The coalition of forces you seem to be opposing are a splinter group concerned with using it for some purpose, which MI6 is aware of and are in the process of thwarting." Now it's Freddie's time to look mistrusting again.

"You said he was *off* and not listening, *Maisie*. Can this computer be trusted?" he asks.

"Yeah - I do wonder sometimes," I reply. "Anton. I thought we were off comms when your red light was off?" I ask, annoyed.

"That is correct. I was doing a background search of the DGSE, and I found out about Frederick's father and his involvement in tracking down this information." Freddie shakes his head.

"Is there nothing this computer does not know?" Freddie asks.

"I am sorry; he is a pain in the butt, but… a useful source of information," I reply.

"Also, I am instructed to keep you safe Maisie," Anton continues. I nod in agreement.

"So far, so good, although his methods are a bit suspect," I say.

Freddie points out where Olga's car is going. 'Place d Armes' Car Park seems to be the destination. We pull around and the full grandeur of this palace hits my eyes. It looks like an old building on steroids, stretching out both ways as far as I can see. I scan the car park and check where they have parked up and tell Freddie to pull past and away from them.

"*IN HERE* - this should be fine. We are out of their line of sight." Freddie slides this beauty into a generous space and kills the engine. He looks across at me. I'm trying to read that expression. Is he scared or just wanting something to eat? I smile and squeeze his hand.

"Thank you so much for trusting me, Freddie. I know I'm a bit crazy, but I'm hoping this will be over soon. You can sit and wait here. I am going to follow them around and check out what they are up to."

He fixes his gaze at me and holds both hands out to me. I give mine. He squeezes them and pulls me close. We kiss gently and his breath is warm and sweet. I feel a tingle rise up my back, and I pull him back for another kiss. I am feeling such a tug at my heart. I could stay here and forget about all this and just run away with him. *BUT*... I know I must finish what I've started.

"Stay here and be safe Freddie, my gorgeous boy. I'll text you when I'm coming back," I say and smile, gathering my gadgets bag.

Anton said it would be useful. I check my suit is in there and rummage around the other stuff neatly packed in the side pockets. Freddie grabs one of my hands.

"Please come back in one piece. I want to kiss all of you one day."

I find myself grimacing without meaning to and my face blushing. I slap him gently around the face.

"Yeah, well; dream on Freddie boy," I say, smirking.

I press the door release and it slides up as quiet as a summer breeze. I bob down and blow him a kiss. It's a huge wrench, but I must check what Olga and Lee are up to and end this.

28 - The Hall of Mirrors

Now, to work out how to get through the gates as I have no ticket. Also, due to the upscaled security, I am uncertain how to get my backpack full of assassin goodies through with me. I look around and watch the crowds gathering to present their tickets. Hmm... a suitable distraction is needed.

I pick on a gullible family group and stand calmly behind them, breaking into a can of coke. I notice a security man standing alongside a soldier, chatting about their boules match from the other night or the latest football score. I don't know, but they seem suitably uninterested in me or anyone else.

I shuffle along with my chosen group and try to blend in. I spot Olga and Lee about twenty people ahead and duck my head, throwing my hood over. My eyes are frozen on their every move as I feel my assassin mode kicking in. I don't see any of the so-called DGSE anywhere, so I have discounted them from this operation. They must be busy going somewhere else.

My group is closer to the gate now, so I focus on my next move. The art of distraction is something I learnt with Olga, after years of making it easier for her to enter a building, administer the death blow to a mark, or just to make a suitable exit. As I am older than I look, I can usually get away with it. Here we go. The ticket people are checking the bags and scanning the tickets. My heart slows as I concentrate. Everything morphs into slow motion, the usual way I cope with these situations.

The family walks through. I stride forward and lurch to the side, throwing my bag onto the nearest kid. Rolling to one side, I force a convulsion, frothing at the mouth. The first to respond is the mother of the group and quickly strides over to me. She is speaking urgently in German, I think, as more people gather around, while anxious ticket checkers hold back the onlookers. I keep the pretence for as long as I can; the coke can only last so long, issuing like some sort of chemical experiment out of my mouth and nose.

Another concerned man comes across and waves people away. He appears to be a first aider. A stretcher is rushed over to me as I wave my arms around like a wild creature. The family I have chosen for this charade is acting according to my scam and gathers my bag and follows me to the side of the gates, along to a building, probably a first aid room.

I am swiftly carried and placed on a bed and a woman is talking softly to me in French. I stare vacantly at the ceiling trying not to break into a smile. The family is hovering at the door, probably asking if I'm ok. The French lady is temporarily distracted, so I glance around the room, checking where my bag is and any exit route.

I see an open window which leads into the gardens. The first aider glances back to me so I continue my frothing and groaning, although my mouth is running out of anything to spit out. She turns away again. *Now*. I must move quickly. I swiftly roll off the bed and skip towards the youngest of the family who strangely has been given the charge of looking after my bag. She stares at me and is about to point when I wink at her and grab my bag.

"*Danke*," I whisper, winking again. She instinctively understands my ruse and winks in return. I think she will be a great con artist herself one day! I quickly sling my bag out the window and follow by a leapfrog over the bed. It unfortunately clatters as it rolls to one side, leaving the first aider shouting, and the rest of the family bemused, I guess, as to my unorthodox exit. In any case, I roll onto a gravel path, grab my bag and run, with the first aider shouting into empty air.

Scanning the outside of this huge palace, I feel it's going to be difficult to track Olga down; I am wondering where to start. I have lost them from the entrance and so I must trace around the outside and I'm already getting tired from jogging.

"Anton. Have you got eyes on Olga and Lee?" I ask, breathless.

"It would appear they are wandering through the palace and observing the masterpieces," he replies. Oh, how lovely!

Perhaps Freddie was right, and they are spending some downtime here. I can't get out of my mind though, all that has happened recently. There are too many loose ends, and they are worryingly converging here, so I can't accept that Olga is just being a tourist. Maybe a *terrorist*, after this revelation of dirty bombs. But this doesn't sound like the stuff she would get into. Unless the data on this stone holds a healthy price tag. I know what she is like where money is concerned. So, is this dragging her into a greater danger than even she is used to?

I continue to run around the edge of the palace looking for an entrance that doesn't have a steward who will suspect me of something. Anton has recommended that I get into the combat suit in case anything kicks off, so I'm searching for a toilet to change in. Eventually, I find an entrance and sneak in behind a larger group of Asian tourists taking photos of everything, including me, (which I could do without). Finally, extracting myself from this happy crowd, I find a loo and get on with my changing.

Slipping my regular clothes over the top, I instantly feel energised and ready for a fight. I'm wearing my hoodie as I don't want any CCTV to pick me up on anyone's feed, as I know from Anton's ability to hack, that would be a mistake.

I move like a ghost through the vast corridors lined with statues and paintings. The floor is slippery from centuries of polishing and my Converse trainers squeak as I try to be invisible, drifting in behind regular groups of tourists. Anton has informed me that Olga and Lee are approaching a long gallery known as the 'Hall of Mirrors' and he kindly gives me the directions on the phone.

Weaving through this great building of opulence gives me the creeps to be honest. I think of all the wealth that is tied up in this one building. No wonder the French revere it so much. I could do with a small percentage of it and get a nice condo in Santorini or Italy and then retire from all this nonsense.

Having turned towards this hallway, I feel like I'm in a river wading against the current as the bustling crowds are walking the other way. I keep my head low as I don't want to draw attention from anyone, except the occasional shoulder bump which makes me feel agitated.

I hear music echoing through the rooms. It sounds like some classical stuff. A strange tingling races up my back and I wonder if this could have been something my mum and dad would have liked. Drawing closer, I can hear people clapping and feet tapping on parquet flooring. Must be a concert or something. Turning the corner into a long hall, I see men and women dressed in costumes, with long wigs, dancing in some old style. This is what they've come to watch? Bizarre!

I gently push by other observers and gaze down the room. I see why this place has its name. The walls are inlaid with mirrors all the way down one side, reflecting the dancers making the event look twice as large. What a perfect place for a girl to do her hair! The chandeliers drape from the ceiling like crystal waterfalls frozen in time and space, sparkling with the sunlight pouring through the windows. Impressive.

Trying not to get distracted by all the gold and dancers, I scan around the hall to pick out Olga and Lee. Right at the other end I spot them. I weave in between people to get a clearer view. Someone pushes past me, and I stop myself from giving a mouthful when I glance up and see who I didn't expect. The man from the street; the meeting with Lee, he's here, *now*! I knew it. This has got to be more than a sightseeing gig.

I watch him slip down the mirrored side of the hall as he nods, catching the eye of Olga. They move in obedience down the same side, much to the annoyance of some of the dancers. Reaching the same point, the man opens a mirrored door, and they disappear inside. Ok, where does that lead to?

"Anton. They have just gone through a doorway in the mirrors. Do you know where that goes?" I whisper. He comes back with a negative.

"It is not a recognised entrance or exit and my feed shows nothing behind those mirrors except stonework. Be careful. It may be a secret passageway," he says, piquing my curiosity.

"Well, that means they *are* planning something. I'm going to have to go in, aren't I? If you can't see or hear anything, then, old style it has to be." Anton doesn't sound convinced, but I reassure him that I've been in situations like this before.

"You really don't have to get it all worked out beforehand, Anton. In my line of work, you have to learn to improvise," I say, trying not to get disgruntled.

Scanning down the mirrors, I estimate my chances of getting there without toppling one of the dancers or getting caught up in their 17th Century gyrations as 50/50. The music is climbing to a crescendo, so I make my move. I shove past the remaining sightseers and scoot down the mirrored side. My backpack strap unfortunately catches on a dress of one of the dancers, sending her spinning like a top towards me. I can't resist. I catch her before she falls and then do an impromptu waltz with her, before throwing her back into the arms of a grumpy looking male dancer. It sends a ripple of laughter around the hall, so I quickly bow to the audience and disappear through the mirror.

Instantly, the darkness closes in on me. My eyes take a moment or two to adjust. This reminds of a mine we had to escape through in India.

***

We had to dispatch an Asian guy who set himself up as a guru, controlling not only a yogi following but under the surface enslaving thousands to work in mines and the sex trade across the north of the country. Olga had done the dispatch in a vat of molten lead (why she had to be so extreme about this one I'm not sure, except as I mentioned, you must improvise with whatever is at hand!)

We were faced with a tricky route out of the mines, tracing miles underground. Olga was *not* happy about being in a hot and enclosed space. We were dehydrated and tired, but we had to keep going. I could hear the avalanche of hitmen chasing us down. Close to the exit, I did that thing you should never do in a tunnel. Light a match, or in this case strike my flint. The gases that had accumulated down there raged into a furnace scorching my hair and bum. I could not sit down for days without it stinging. It also had the desired effect of stopping the chasers in their tracks. I guess they didn't have much fun sitting down either.

***

Slowly my sight is recovering, and I see steps leading away parallel with the wall. I whisper to Anton to check he's still with me.

"Yes, I have communications with you. I would proceed with caution. This hidden area is not shown on any data I have, so we are blind," he says, *so* reassuringly.

"Yes, *ok*. Stop trying to freak me out. I'll put on the night vision head covering to see if I can trace any heat signatures."

"I have some other updates on the DGSE also. The van you spotted was registered with the military but has been recorded as stolen. Did you see any signs of them at the gate?"

"Nope, and so I've ignored them. I suppose you could watch what's happening around here, so I'm not surprised by anything else?"

"Of course. I am ready and will alert you to any danger." Thanks Anton. You're a peach.

This passageway leads downwards, and I sense it is going underneath the hallway. If this wasn't so highly charged and dangerous, I could enjoy exploring old secret passageways, feeling excited over what you are about to find. Today, I'm quite apprehensive about this. I pick up nothing on the night vision but steadily step downwards on gritty stone steps, occasionally sliding. Does this suit have enhanced audio too I wonder? Anton says it does.

Activating the app, I can faintly hear talking and crunching of walking. These steps must go down forever. It's like descending into the bowels of a dank beast. I can smell musty air and there is a cold draft. I do hope this doesn't lead to water; the memory of that well is far too recent. The stairs take a sharp right turn, and the floor now flattens out. Still no orange glow of bodies or light, but the talking is clearer. They are speaking French again, which is annoying.

"Anton. Can you do a translation thing here?" I ask.

"Of course," he replies, as smugly as a computer can.

"Listen to what I pick up and relay it back to me." I stand still so it doesn't interfere with the feed. After a few seconds he reports his findings.

"They are discussing the release of documents which are related to a separatist group called "La Restauration de la Fierté de France"."

"Who are they?" I ask.

"They are a group formed after the continued breakup of the EU and their objectives are to force the government into establishing French pride, harkening back to the empire days."

"Oh, so they are the ones who are trying to get a dirty bomb together, I guess. So, not the official French authorities. But I can't understand what I have to do with all this and why the sapphire is so important?"

"A terrorist group such as this do not require any logical reasoning to validate their objectives, Maisie. That's why MI6 have long attempted to keep these sorts of people at bay. Your mother and father established many ties with countries to prevent rogue groups destabilising the world. This why you have to continue their work."

O-M-G!

"Look, don't start that again. I have one aim and only one. At the end of this, I am out, finished, do you hear? This is not the time to be dragging my ass into espionage and all that crap." Silence again, as I quietly fume.

The talking has also stopped, along with any crunching. So, they must be closer. The darkness draws me ever forward, my heart racing. I feel my hands tighten and my legs are tense. If this were a horror movie, I'd expect a ghoul or two to suddenly jump out at me. There are enough recesses in these walls to hide an army of them. What could this place be for? An escape for the kings and queens of old? Anyway, I must concentrate, or I'll end up being history too. I hear a creak and groaning noise, then a buzz of electronics. They must have reached a door into another room.

The floor takes another turn to the left and my night vision suddenly makes everything as bright as day. I flip it back as it's too bright. I stare at a group of people staring back at me. *Oh shit*. That was not good surveillance. Am I screwed? A flash and pain strike through my shoulders and along my legs, forcing me to the ground. One of the group marches towards me. I barely have any control as the taser is making my body rigid. I have enough energy to look upwards into the eyes of… *arrrgh*.

29

"The vestment does not make the monk".
"L'habit ne fait pas le moine"

The smell of burning material makes me choke and splutter as I try to move my achy limbs. My vision is all blurry and the light is hurting my brain. Again, I try to move my arms, but they seem to be dislocated from my will, fixed in place, numb and unresponsive. *What is going on?* I shake my head, trying to get some clarity. Blinking again and again, my eyes are forming a sort of image. I shudder as the figure in front of me comes into focus. *Not again!*

"Wakey, wakey, Maisie Greene, time to tell me everything you have seen," Blondie says, trying a lyrical verse. With a sneer stretching across her bitch face, she glares at me. Strength is returning to my arms and legs, and I try to move again. No good, I still can't. I glance down and now see the reason. Straps are wrapped around every part of me. I look like I'm ready for the electric chair or resembling a trussed-up Christmas turkey. My face morphs into a snarl and I spit at her. I miss by a mile, unfortunately. She laughs and strides across to a console.

"Well, if you're in that mood we will have to quieten your temper down," she says. I have a moment of anxiety as she flips a switch. *What is she doing?* I don't have to wait.

"Arrrr ... arrr... *SHIT... what are you doin... ARRRGH!!*" The pain is excruciating. It rips through my body, exposing all my nerves to fire. I feel myself slipping away. A splash of water wakes me up.

"Now then, we can't have you falling asleep, not while I have some fun with you. Now, tell me where it is, and this can all over within an instant. NO more pain - no more Maisie-*fucking*-Greene. Tell me you little bitch - I haven't got all day. You have wasted my time already. Shame I didn't get to blow your boyfriend to bits. Would have made a lovely addition to the Eiffel Tower. So, what will it be?" she says, continuing her verbal diarrhoea.

I shake my head to get the water and hair stuck to my face out of my eyes. I stare as hard as I can, as there is nothing else to do. I am saying nothing. No matter what she does to me, I'm not giving up what my parents died for. She shakes her head and flicks the switch again. *God, give me strength*. This time the pain is so bad I just squeal and writhe around like a spike is being slowly pushed up my spine. Oh God, I don't know how much of this I can take.

She steps away from the console and waltzes over to me, a sick grin across her hideous face. I hang my head as I've no strength left to hold it up in defiance. Her hand jabs under my chin, forcing my eyes up to hers. I see two of her now; it was bad enough just seeing one.

"Come on, we know who you are. Olga's attempt at hiding you didn't work. The poor little child, defenceless, without parents and no future. She was too soft. If it had been my way, the wolves would have been let loose to finish you off. Tell me… when did you find out it was her that killed your parents? Must have been quite a moment. Wish I'd been there. I would have loved to have seen the truth dawning across your innocent little face." She slaps me hard, making me cough and spray blood.

I force a tear back. I'm not showing her any weakness. I must be as strong and defiant as possible. Again, I stare hard at her. I'm trying to think what to do, but my mind is a mess. *What did she mean Olga hid me?* I cough again, blood pouring down my chin. I hear the scraping of feet walking into the room. They stay behind me and 'bitch-face' Chase wanders over. I can just hear them talking, but my hearing must be damaged cos' it's muffled. She strides back again and looks perturbed for her. I gather up some strength and shout.

"And I know who you are too, Harmony 'shit-face' Chase," I spit out with as much venom as I can. It seems to have a welcome effect; for a moment she hesitates, a look of recognition of an old life covered up. She flips the switch again. I don't think I was wise, but it was worth it

- until the pain wrenches me so much, I want my skin to peel off. I let out a scream and I fade into darkness.

***

The next shaft of blurry light streaming in through my eyes brings more disappointment. The figure in front of me is another one I hate so much right now. Olga stares at me, pursing her lips, either through annoyance or feeling sorry for me. I shake my head.

"What do *you* want? Is it your turn to torture me? *Bastard!*" She takes a glance around and up to a CCTV camera in the room.

Approaching me swiftly, she grabs me by the shoulders. Looking into her eyes feels weird after all that I have found out about her. At one time I could read that face, knew what she was thinking, and know how to help her. All I feel now is hatred and anger. Yet, I notice in the corner of her eye a tear forming. It rolls slowly down her cheek, into her mouth. Is this another ploy? Bad agent, good agent. Let's see which one works. Break my will and then they win. I shake my head.

"Not going to happen, Olga. You are not winding me round your finger anymore. We are not together, we are different. Always have been, but now I understand why. You are a traitor, a charlatan, a deep fake. I put my trust in you all these years and yet you manipulated me into thinking you were there for me. Do you know how messed up that sounds? I cannot forgive you for this - for anything. Get it over with. I'm sick of being in the same world with you." She doesn't say a word and again looks up at the camera.

I don't want to look at her, I am so pissed off right now. I just want out. Out of here, out of life. Yet what can I do? I am stuffed, left to their deranged will. Olga walks past me, and I hear a door closing with a bang. Thank goodness, a bit of peace. I stare at the wall ahead of me and to the console. If only I could get Anton to deactivate it or blow it up. *Anton!* I wonder if he can respond. I don't know what they have done to the suit I am wearing. Does it still work? I whisper.

"Anton, can you hear me?" I wait. "Can you hear me? Please respond." I wait again.

A puff of smoke rises from my shoulder. Perhaps all the volts Blondie has zapped me with has blown the suit completely. This is not good. What is the plan? I was foolish to come into this without a plan. My usual preparation has left me and I'm suffering because of it. I try to look around the room, which gives me no encouragement. It is a blank cave with just this torture box in front of me. I can't even shuffle the chair around because it's fixed to the ground.

I glance at my wrist to see if my watch is still intact. Again, it looks like it's toast. I'm wondering if all my stuff has been ransacked. I can feel myself wilting. I can do nothing, and no one can help. Then, another noise makes me tense up. The door is slowly opened. Who is it this time? Lee? Is he coming to do a comedy act, maybe a little dance? I wait for what seems ages and no one appears.

"Whoever the fuck you are, show yourself. It's not a freak show. Or are you scared? Come on, where I can see you." I hear shuffling and a knife appears waving beside my head.

Whoa! I wasn't expecting the knife clown from the airport again. The knife wavers as if it's undecided what to do. I feel it move down my back and then up sharply. I expected it to penetrate my skin, but then remembered the suit is still tear proof, so should give me protection. I feel a release, the pressure of the bindings allowing me to breathe deeply again. *Are they cutting me free?*

I push my body forward and raise my shoulders, trying to get the blood flowing. They continue to cut, and I lurch forward as I can't control my legs. Collapsing on the floor, I spin around to see who is helping me. I see a figure in the shade, but my vision is still blurry, and I don't recognise them. They push a finger to their mouth and beckon me to follow. I try to stand but stumble. I have little coordination as my body has been shocked so much there is barely any strength, but I will myself to move. The door opens and the figure scuttles down the corridor as I look both ways to check this isn't a trap. No one is around. I force my legs to move and follow.

Who is this person? Am I putting my life in the hands of a stranger? In any case, it's got to be better than being electrocuted by Harmony Chase. Come to think of it, how could her parents give her such a sweet sickly name? At least my sense of humour is returning as I continue to stumble down this dimly lit rock corridor. Another door halts our progress, and the figure punches a code into the lock. It opens with a whine and groan, as if it hasn't been oiled for a century. Ahead I see a brighter light and continue to follow like a desperate monkey seeking bananas.

"Where are we going?" I ask.

I can now see it is a male and he pushes his finger up to his lips again. Can't he speak? Or is he French and doesn't speak any English? Whatever the reason, I feel like freedom is ahead of me and I feel the rush of adrenaline again as we near the light. Another door this time, looking modern and half windowed, is opened and he ushers me through. I stand in a spacious room, which must be part of the palace. It's high ornate ceilings and chandeliers lift my spirits and I breath in deeply, as if coming out of water. He beckons me to sit down on one of the plush chairs. I am quite happy to do that, as I feel the need for some comfort.

"Attendez ici s'il vous plaît," he says, and strides off to another door exiting the room.

So, he *can* talk. I'm not sure what he said, but I think he means for me to stay here. This feels so surreal. I've just been effectively tortured to an inch of my life and now I'm sitting in someone's exquisite lounge. I am completely confused.

The silence bounces around in my throbbing head, like a tennis ball on speed. I keep shaking it to get my thinking straight. I vaguely pick out someone talking but can't locate where from. Slowly, my ears are returning to normal, and I hear something about standing close to a window. I get up and stagger towards a sunlit one looking out onto beautiful, manicured lawns and hedges. Never been into gardening much, but I can appreciate the skill that's gone into that. I hear the voice again, a little clearer. Is that Anton?

"Hey, Anton, can you hear me?"

"Yes," replies a muffled garbled voice. "You are charging the suit up by solar so stay there! I lost all comms for a while. Are you ok?" Well, what do I say? "I am so sorry that you had to endure that alone. Where are you now?" he asks urgently.

"In someone's very posh lounge. I don't think it's part of the regular palace tour. Probably private quarters. The weird thing is a man came and set me free. I have no idea what is happening now. Can you see where Olga and Lee are? What about the Harmonious bitch?" He tells me that none of them are on his radar. Hmmm... so what about this man who is a diplomat?

"Did you see the man that brushed past me in the Hall of Mirrors? He was the one that Lee went to see, the one I saw entering a diplomatic office. He led the two of them down into this dungeon." Anton tells me the profile of this man is classified, not even his hacking can get a fix on him.

"This is deep shit don't you think?" I say, wondering if I should just get going and escape while I have a chance. Without realising, someone had walked into the room. I hear a gravelly voice.

"Yes, it is deeper than you think, Maisie Greene." I turn and stare at the man who is so highly classified, no one knows who he is.

"*L'habit ne fait pas le moine,*" he reels off, like some poet from a French parody. His swirling hand movements leave me feeling semi-amused. I hope he is going to explain.

"'The habit does not make the monk'," he continues. "Difficult to work out who is who in this world of charlatans, don't you think, Maisie?" He is not making any sense.

"What are you talking about? What monks and what habits are we into?" I say with as much aggravation as I can give and scan the room for the best exit from this French lesson.

"You see Maisie, your parents were expert authors of death and life. On the surface they seemed genuine cultured people. Your mother, a talented opera singer; your father, an intelligent technician." I am wondering where this is going. I have heard so many sides to their story. I think this is another version which I do not want to listen to, but I am compelled.

"I had many dealing with them, even shared in their missions from time to time. But one of their failings was that they couldn't bend the rules, allow a bit of slack to ensure that colleagues' lives were saved. They became dangerous to work with. I feel a little background information would be useful for you to understand our concerns with yourself." At this, I grimace. What has this to do with me as a five-year-old?

"One particular mission was to secure the remnants of cold war documentation relating to chemical and biological warfare. As you can appreciate, to allow that to circulate in the open market would cause any country to be nervous. So, it was their job to ensure that the information remained buried, secure from any terrorist group, or rogue nation.

They were aligned with another couple working for MI6 to ascertain how to capture this information and return it to the UK for safe keeping. However, there were complications and the deal with the current owners went wrong. The only way was to force the surrender of the documentation and ensure that it didn't get on the internet. The couple your parents were working with got caught in the crossfire when they didn't need to be. They were killed, Maisie, because of your parents' ineptness."

I must stop myself from both yawning and getting angry about how my parents are being portrayed again. I hold up my hand.

"Just a minute. So, what has that got to do with me? They were killed *as well*. So, what's the deal?" I say, getting more annoyed with each breath.

"The deal, Maisie bitch, is that they were *my* parents that were killed by *yours*. Then they chose to hide those documents with *you*," says the voice I have grown so much wanting to strangle. I turn and Chase walks in looking as if a good swipe around her smiling face would do her a world of good.

"We learnt that the sapphire they left you hides that information, and *we* want it. It is time for us to get a good retirement package and leave the world to rot in hell." What a lovely summary of her selflessness.

I hear a clatter from outside the room as a group bustle in with someone with a hood over their head. I back away anxious about how this is turning out. It looks like a brigade from this DGSE has brought someone in.

"Now we have a bargaining chip with you. Give us the sapphire and the code for breaking it, or we shoot," she says pointing her Glock at whoever this is. I'm getting more agitated and whisper to Anton.

"How is this situation supposed to play out, Anton? What should I do?"

"There is no need to whisper Maisie, your 'Anton' is merely a puppet of mine, to draw you closer to us," says the man.

I shudder and gasp, nearly falling over backwards. What? He's not autonomous? Not something my father created for me.

"What do you mean?" I say, feeling my eyes widening.

"As I said, *L'habit ne fait pas le moine.*"

Chase laughs and stands closer to the hooded figure. I look down at their feet. They are high laced up black boots. No…No…*NO. It can't be.*

"So, a second chance to score a bullseye, or should I say - *a Frederick's eye,*" Chase cackles.

I step back next to the window. Is Anton really a puppet? How do I know what's real anymore? I try to think. I must find a plan to get Freddie and me out of here alive. I glance around the room. I have five soldiers with automatic weapons: Blondie with a Glock at Freddie's head and I'm in a room with no easy way out. I force a decision.

"Freddie, I know it's you under there. Where did you keep my other bags?"

"I...I brought them with me because I saw you have fit at the entrance and I followed you in... sorry..." he says, his voice barely discernible because of his nerves. Blondie looks across at one of the soldiers who has my bags. She nods to him to bring them over to her.

"Don't worry Freddie. We *will* get out of here," I say to try and calm him. I turn to Chase.

"It's in the side pocket where the makeup bag is," I say firmly. Blondie rummages around, pulling out my mum's beautiful dress, throwing it on the floor with little respect. This alone raises my anger levels. I hear a vague voice coming in from the suit balaclava.

"This is Anton. My system has been overridden by some unknown host. If I have given incorrect information, I apologise. You have the suit. I am going offline so I will not interfere with what you are about to do."

"What? I can't trust you, so I'm not listening," I whisper back, making the man laugh.

"Yes, I know, but this is where you - *improvise*," he says. I almost think he was giving me a wink. "Goodbye and good luck."

I watch as Blondie pulls out the necklace and holds it up like an athlete who's won a tournament. The man comes over and gazes at it.

"Such beauty holds so much more than reflected light. Now Maisie, *the code*," he demands. I look straight at him.

"I wish I knew. I have been trying to get it to work but failed. I honestly don't know how it works," I say, failing to hold back a sneer. Blondie shoots a death stare at me.

"I wouldn't play the stupid card with me you silly little girl. How much do you want to see Freddie boy's head splattered into a thousand bits? You are testing me too far." I flinch as I know she is not bluffing. What can I do? *I don't know what it is.*

"Maisie. It would be something that your mother said a thousand times over you as a child. It's bound to be something simple, come on. Please do as Harmony asks. We don't want to clean up the mess it will cause here," he says.

I try to recall anything, but what happened to my memory before Olga I have not got a clue. On cue, she and Lee enter the room, looking pensive.

"What is going on here? I thought you were letting her go," Olga demands.

"Well, the deal was for the sapphire and the code. We have the jewel but no code. So, unless you have any other ideas then we must force it out of her," Blondie says, sneering. Olga looks at me, while Lee is taking a wide walk around behind the man.

"Come on Maisie. You should know what it was. You are good at watching my back and improvising." At that phrase, my heart jumps.

It's what she always said to me on a mission: '*Maisie G, you are my talisman*'. I look at her and narrow my eyes. I watch as hers narrow too. Her twitchy eye begins to flutter. This brings a tingle up and down my back. I morph into my slow-motion mode as I calculate the next move.

"Combat ready," I say out loud. My suit, now fully charged, forces my tired limbs to prepare for action. The man talks to his watch. He looks concerned for some reason.

"Has Anton shut you out?" I say in a girly voice. Rage runs across his face. Blondie snatches the necklace and storms across to me.

"Speak the code or he dies!"

"*Maisie G - I am the talisman*," I say calmly at the sapphire. Light starts to shine from it, and I can see that the projection is running a program. The man marches over to me and snatches it back.

"Quickly. We must place it on the reader to capture the information." He turns to a box where he places it in a clasp. The projection is now spewing out its secrets as the computer sucks it up like a blueberry milkshake.

While all this excitement over the stone's miraculous jumping into life is happening, I watch with interest at what Olga and Lee are doing. They have taken up positions like Olga and I would have done in the past when surrounded by seemingly overwhelming odds. The soldiers are quietly stationed by the door, Harmony (I can't call her that!) 'bitch' face is mesmerised by the stone and the man is looking smugly at me.

"Well done, Maisie. It took a simple action to save your friend's life. Now unfortunately we are going to have to say goodbye, as I have work to complete with our group," he says.

"Oh, with 'La Restauration de la *Fart* de France'?" I'm deliberately mispronouncing on purpose. He laughs.

"Oh no, no... that was all made up. A little misinformation I fed your computer chum. No, this is purely financial. One which Harmony and I will benefit from. Thank you so much Maisie. It's been a long time coming but now, as we say, *au revoir*." He nods at Chase and the soldiers. He walks off through another door with the computer and Chase glances between me and Freddie.

"So, now Maisie? What will it be? You or him first?" Blondie waves her Glock at Freddie. I was hoping that the suit would be combat ready, but it doesn't feel right. I stare at her then at the soldiers. Improvise, that's what I must do.

"You do realise that the data on that stone will give you nothing but drivel. I have made sure that it was corrupted," I say straight faced. Chase gives me a hard stare.

"You are bluffing. There is no way to corrupt it until it was released, and I know you didn't do that before today. So, time to settle a score." I glare at her. This can't end with her shooting us both in the head.

"Before we get to you, a few loose ends to clear up," she says and sneers. Before I can react, she points her gun at Olga and fires and then shoots Lee in the chest. I am frozen, my eyes not believing what she has done. That was not supposed to happen.

A tear rolls down my face as I watch Olga sink to the floor, blood dripping from her gut. *NO!* My response is not what I expected. Up until now I wanted to kill her. But as I see her life draining away, it breaks my heart. I wipe away tears falling faster than I can blink. My nose is blocked, mixed with blood and snot, as I nearly choke. Chase turns and sneers waving her weapon in my face.

"They had it coming to them. After all, she did kill your parents, so justice is done. Just one other thing I must deliver now, and that's my own personal revenge for my parents. First, though, I want to see you suffer, like I did when they died in my arms." She points the gun at Freddie's head. I grimace as I see the soldiers pointing their automatics at me. Oh God… what do I do now?

30 - The Bitter Ending

I stare at Olga lying on her side, bleeding all over the parquet flooring, feeling like my own life is draining away too. This is not the reaction I expected after my pent-up hatred for her. I wipe away the tears streaming down my bloody face. Sprawled on his back, Lee is groaning and gasping. Wrenching my vision away from them, I glare at Blondie.

She is grinning, thinking she has all the cards in a winning hand. The soldiers now have their green lasers trained on me, one holding Freddie by the shoulder, making me hesitate over what to do. With no Anton to advise or give backup, I feel exposed. I try to force a reaction, a diversion, but I am numb. Chase snakes over to me.

"Just us now. So, what shall we do? Have a game of chess or a drink? I know...what if we see if you can beat me in a brawl? I think I would like that. Olga has trained you pretty well, but I was always the one to beat her in hand to hand." I stare hard. She and Olga worked together?

"What... what do you mean, did you train with her?" I ask, anxiously glancing at her.

"*Ha* - so much she has hidden from you. She was good at hiding things. We didn't realise it was you she had adopted until recently. But now at least we can at last proceed with our plans," she says, scowling. "I knew her from the early days of our work with the agency. Both young and ambitious, we wanted the same. To be efficient and effective. Except, Olga always had the weight of her parents' death hanging over her. It scrambled her brain."

"When your parents killed mine, I began to understand why Olga reacted the way she did. Always looking for revenge. I didn't have that luxury. As far as I was concerned, there was no one I could get that with, until I found out about *you*." Her face sneers and she whips her gun across my face and down on Freddie's head. I grimace and stop myself from lurching forwards.

Chase walks over to gaze at Lee and Olga. Without hesitation, she cocks her head and shoots again, Lee's head shattering on the floor. I can't believe what I witnessed; it shocks me to the core, my body and brain freezing. I hear my heart thumping in my ears, as the tension is building up in my body like a restless volcano. I feel myself shaking trying to get myself into fight mode but completely drained.

Olga moans with mournful sounds across to Lee's lifeless body. She is suffering bigtime. Freddie is also groaning on the floor, lying in a foetus position. I grimace and force some inspiration from a hidden depth, remembering something that Anton told me. Chase now wanders across to Olga. I must stop her from finishing the job. I scan the soldiers and see they are on some sort of comms system. This had better work.

"Activate EMP," I say as a whisper, but scared I won't get a second chance and it's louder than I wanted. Piercing eyes look through balaclavas wondering what I've said. Chase spins around and glares at me. Then, as I pray, the soldiers start a merry dance, pulling out their earpieces and grabbing at the electronics strapped across their bodies as the pulse from my suit fuses all the electronics in the room. Lights shatter, sending showers of glass. Chase pulls her earpiece out and swears as it crackles, the shock distracting her. The suit gives the instruction that power is now at zero, the pulse draining any other functions, so I must react quickly.

I jump across a chair and leap at the group of soldiers, now in disarray. The first one I contact with my foot is sent spiralling into the others. I grab a weapon and fire, aiming low to disable them. I kick away the remaining weapons and roll across the line of fallen soldiers making sure they all stay down with a series of kicks and punches to the head. I catch Chase in the corner of my eye aiming her Glock at me.

I instinctively duck and hide behind one of the fallen men. Her shot embeds itself in his chest. Another bullet ricochets off a helmet, another off some body armour. I see her marching relentlessly towards me, firing as quickly as the Glock allows. I glance upwards and fire at the chandelier above her. It crashes down splintering and shattering over her head as she crumples underneath it and yells, much to my satisfaction.

I push the soldier off me and lurch towards where Olga is lying. My heart is thumping, and I feel a well of emotion gushing through my face. I nurse her head in my arms and push some clothing over her wound. In typical style, she tries to wave me off, but I persist. Her face is ashen, sprinkled with red, her eyes losing that resilience I am so familiar with. Her hand rises to gently stroke my cheek, and her weak smile flickers.

"You *are* my talisman, Maisie… always looking after me, as I have done for you," she splutters. I feel a warmth welling up and hot tears drip onto her bloody chest. "I tried to get you to safety, but I should have known you wouldn't stay away once you found out the truth. Lee and I tried our best to keep you out of this. We didn't mean you any harm. He was the one in the agency that knew the truth about you; the only one who I could trust," she continues, coughing.

"But why Olga? Why did you kill my parents and then adopt me?"

"Maisie…they loved you so much…I had worked my way into their confidence to find out about their work and stop them. The agency wanted the information they held about them and other agencies… people who would be useful to control. But as I got to know them, I was torn over the whole mission. They were decent people, fulfilling a much-needed role in the world. It put me to shame with the sort of operations I was into.

They knew a hit was out on them and asked me to make sure that you were saved if anything went wrong. They trusted me with you, Maisie. They begged me to look after you in case of their deaths. I became like a Godmother to you," she says, now breaking up and crying.

I can't believe what she is saying, and it causes a wave of emotion to crash down on my head. I am melting under this revelation.

"I couldn't do it. I was the one given the task of killing them. How could I do that, knowing they were trusting me with their daughter? I told the agency that someone else had to do it. Chase was working for MI6 at the time but was also recruited by the agency.

She was always more ruthless than me. She was the one that forced me to get on and complete the mission or she would expose my faltering. So, under threat of isolation and death, I went ahead. Unknown to her and the agency, I managed to get you to safety before the dispatch. I sent you to an orphanage." At this, I shake my head. It still causes anger to build up in me.

"You still killed my parents, *Olga*! How could you do that?"

"Someone would have done it Maisie, if not me, Chase probably, after killing me first. So, I had little choice. At least you were going to be safe, this is what I consoled myself with." She splutters and blood oozes down the side of her mouth. I shake my head, trying to make any sense out of this puzzle. She turns her head towards me and tries another weak smile.

"You trained well. Marian always wanted you to learn how to look after yourself. James was such an adoring father. He wanted a helper to be there in the hard times to carry on their work. When you told me about Anton, I was shocked and worried that the agency had fooled you, but now I see it was his invention."

"And the house…how did you get that?" I ask.

"The plan was that you had a place where you could find shelter and peace away from this brutal lifestyle. It was left to me, for you. I was hesitant about taking you there in case you remembered anything." She starts to drift. I shake her. I am not losing her even though she is the reason why I am in this mess.

"*No…no* you are *not* dying. We are getting out of here."

I glance to where Freddie is lying. He managed to be wedged under one of the soldiers, moaning about being squashed. I slowly get Olga to her feet, but realise that she has little strength, so I rest her on a chaise long. I run over to Freddie and drag the soldier off him. He moans again.

"Ok... Freddie, you *are* ok. Stop whining." I pull his hood off and his eyes narrow trying to get used to the light. "I need you to help me get Olga to a medic. Come on we need to move fast," I say anxiously, pulling him across to her.

"*Mon Dieu!* All these people are dead!" he says and starts gagging seeing Lee's shattered head.

"Not all... *we* are still alive, but only if we hurray. Hold Olga one side. We will aim for that door over there," I say pointing, through where the man left.

We stagger past Lee's body, crunching on the glass strewn flooring. We barely reach the door as a shot rings out and glances my head. The sting was instant, and I yell. We both turn and see Chase wavering on her knees about to shoot again. Quickly, I push Olga and Freddie through the door.

"*Go...go, get her medical help. I'll sort this out*," I shout urgently. Freddie seems more awake now and urgently helps Olga along the corridor.

I roll back into the room, hiding behind a table with a marble top. I push it over with a more smashing of pots and glass as the contents are thrown. Another shot crashed into the marble and shatters it.

"Another attempt at hiding, Maisie Greene. Well, I think you chose unwisely. This will be very satisfying…finally wiping the Greene gene off the face of the earth," she hisses.

I hear another click and another, followed by another annoyed click. She's out of ammo. I must get to her before she gets a semi-automatic. I wipe away the blood oozing from my wound and glance to where she might go. Predictably, she reaches across for one of the soldier's weapons. I leap to my feet and run at full speed.

Sliding across the floor, I flip her away by kicking her legs, her shoulders bouncing on the shattered glass that litters the floor. She screams as I see some shards are stuck in her back. Quickly I stand up, realising that I have sent one of the weapons closer to her than I wanted. Now I must make a quick decision where to go. I have no weapon close to hand and I'm not sure if this suit will withstand an onslaught of 45mm bullets. There is a door leading off in the opposite direction to where Olga and Freddie have gone. This must be the best route.

I dash towards it as Chase makes a grab for the weapon. I scramble through the door and down a short corridor, finding myself in a section of the Hall of Mirrors. The dance has finished and there are only a few people wandering around. I must clear them away or they will be in danger.

"Everyone out, as quickly as possible," I shout. *"There is a crazy woman with a gun in there - quick!!"* I wasn't sure if anyone spoke English, but it had the desired effect and it sent people running like headless chickens towards the other end.

I join them, running as fast as I can, but then slow down as I hear a repeat blast of shots ring out and the mirrors explode around me in a flash of sparkling shafts of sunlight. I slither to a halt. Chase is sneering and holding another weapon ready to blast me to hell. My only response now is to face her full on. I gulp and pray for deliverance, my grandmother's words ringing in my ears, along with the splintering glass.

Slowly we walk towards each other. She has that bitch face on, where she thinks she is superior, except the glass cuts have gouged her face with multiple cuts and her hair is covered in shards, sparkling in the sunlight, making her look like a grisly fairy.

"We don't want to die, do we Maisie? But today is the day I *shall* get my vengeance *and* satisfaction. I'll make it slow and painful, like it was for my parents. Then you will wish you had been carved up with your parents on that day twelve years ago." She laughs and then fires above my head, crystal waterfalls shattering around me, embedding in my skin.

I scream as the glass shreds one side of my face and blood streams. It makes me stagger to prop myself against a statue. Composing myself, I glare at her.

"Well, let's see what sort of fighter you *really* are," I snarl. "Come on, hand to hand. No weapons, just us. Are you up to it?" I spit out the congealed blood from her earlier thrashing of my face.

The cuts are stinging, and it sends my sight woozy, but I force myself to keep focused. Surprisingly, she throws her weapons down. I gambled on her being too proud to let this opportunity go. It appears to have worked. She flicks her hair back and I hastily tie mine in a glass filled ponytail.

We slowly walk towards each other, assessing our first moves. Each step we take crunches underfoot, amplifying our steps. I see that she is favouring her left leg, possibly injured in the chandelier crush. *Noted*. I am being careful not to show any weakness, although my mind is dull, the pain giving me a banging headache.

We get within striking distance. I keep my eyes fixed on hers. Any flinch and I will launch into my usual Jeet Kune Do. I must remain fluid, keep relaxed, although it's not that easy now to be honest. I watch her circling, adopting a typical street fighter's stance, crude but effective if it catches the opponent off guard. Our eyes are on fire, testing each other's resolve.

Suddenly she launches into an attack, swift and accurate, kicking at my legs and punching my face. I responded too slowly, the kick glancing at my knee, the punch drifting across my nose. *Ouch...* that was painful. I hobble backwards, keeping as light on my feet as possible. Blood begins to dribble into my mouth. I taste the fresh red and spit it out.

Again, I mirror her circling. She throws a dummy punch and follows with a high back kick, aiming for my head. She spins and returns to her stance. It misses. I'm finding my focus is groggy and keep shaking my head. This prompts her to attack with more kicks and punches and I try to parry away as many as possible. This attack leaves her open; in her hurray to disable me she fell short.

I allow my body to bend and wave, watching in slow motion her arm crosses over my head. I thrust my fist sharp and hard against her throat, followed by a swift kick in the groin. She reels backwards, holding her throat, staggering with the force of my kick. Now I see a shock wave rippling through her thinking. I'm not as easy as she was hoping.

"All too hard for you, Harmony? Come on, your age must be slowing you down," I say, giving a painful smile.

"Bitch...you are going to get what's coming," she snarls.

She again launches into a mass of frenzied kicks and punches, forcing me backwards. One kick managed to get through my defence and bashes me hard on the side of head, sending me into a spin. I collapse on the floor, the glass shards jabbing my hands. She marches towards me. I blink focus into my eyes and remember something. I still have my cord and knife.

Quickly I reach down and pull it out. I sidestep a stamp from her foot and slither on glass splinters towards a shattered mirror. I see her running towards me in the myriad of reflections. Turning, I flick out the cord. It whips out, the knife embedding in her throat. A look of horror floods across her eyes. I pull with all my might sideways and the knife does its work. She screams as bright red blood pours down her chest.

She stumbles gripping her neck, flailing as she reaches out to grab me. I push backwards, allowing her collapse. As her knees crunch on the floor, I hear a gurgling sound, making me feel sick. Then she falls forwards, upright shards of the mirror forcing through her torso. I turn away; it's so disgusting.

This is not what I wanted, but the phrase *'Chase despatched'* runs automatically through my mind.

31 - The Hospital

I lean against a golden statue holding the remnants of some glass work and wonder if this hall has ever seen such devastation and death before. I knew that some sort of treaty was signed here, but that's all.

Chase's blood is oozing out from beneath her, creating the effect of stained glass on the shards. I stare at it numb and dazed. Whilst trying to reign in my breathing, sirens begin to screech. It brings my thinking back into sharp focus. Security will be here soon so I must get out quickly. I can't go via the usual exits, so the only way is the door leading to the underground passageway. That should get me away from the commotion. I take a last look at the pathetic body of Harmony Chase.

"I'm truly sorry that my parents caused their deaths. But it had nothing to do with me." What I say sounds like an epitaph.

I am repulsed as she is the only person I have ever needed to kill, face to face. I feel bad to be honest - but good that I won. It was either her or me. My thoughts revert to finding Olga and Freddie, except they are clouded with the horror of Chase's death.

I force myself up and move to the secret door. It's still as dark and uninviting as the first time, but I know where I'm going, so I run down the steps and along the passageways without caring too much. I get to the door that creaked and check that the silent French man isn't lurking around and run to the other door. The chamber appears quiet, and the sleeping soldiers are still in place. Scrambling around the scattered furniture to the door where Freddie left with Olga, I thank Lee as I pass his silent corpse.

It leads me out into a side hallway away from the tourist sections. I follow a blood trail. This must be Olga's. Through a door into a garden area, it takes me along a gravel path and then towards a patch of grass. I frantically search around but the trail ends abruptly, no smears anywhere. What has happened to her?

Holding my head, I feel nauseous and have to sit down. Everything is starting to spin. I hear a droning noise and look around without seeing what it was, my hair getting a life of its own wafting around my face like a hurricane. Looking up I see what is causing it.

A helicopter is gently touching down beside me. This has got to be the police or DGSE or some other group coming to finish me off. To be honest, the way I'm feeling I don't care. My face is stinging with all the wind flicking my hair around and I'm sat in a self-pity party where I am the main guest. I sit crossed legged and hang my head.

A voice shouts over the noise, one I can barely hear. Then, a hand grabs my shoulder. I instinctively catch it and bend it back, whilst twisting the arm and rolling to the side, giving the owner a slingshot over my shoulder. A yell of '*oh mon dieu*' comes from the assailant. I look across at whom I have thrown, and my heart misses a beat.

"*Freddie*...what the hell are you doing... *in a helicopter?*" I ask, surprised.

"*Oww*...I was coming to rescue you...but I think *I am* the one who needs it... *again!*" His expression is both comical and concerned.

"Oh Freddie...I am so sorry... I am wound up like a spring with all the crap we have been through. I was expecting the authorities to take me away."

"Oui...that would have been a good idea. However, I have news of Olga and I am taking you to her...if that is, ok?" His pained expression is priceless.

I nod and reach out a bloodied hand. He takes it and leads me to the chopper. Once inside he gives me headphones and I sit painfully in the bucket seat.

"How did you get this?" I ask, amazed.

"I rang my father and he managed to commandeer one from the military. I told you he still had contacts. He is very interested in *you* though." At this, I feel like hitting him, even though I am grateful as well.

"We are heading for the hospital, as Olga needed emergency surgery. I think you need some attention too."

He looks me up and down and holds out a hand. I give him a wave and slump back into the seat. I don't want to talk now, it's all too much effort. I close my eyes and drift into a half dream world and flinch when I see Chase and the slit in her throat. The noise of the rotors keeps sending me asleep, but it isn't too long before I feel my stomach rise as we fall downwards to wherever we are landing.

"We are here Maisie, *wake up*," I hear Freddie shouting.

My eyes feel like they have been pinned shut with staples. The effort of getting up is so painful. I am feeling every cut and bruise. He leads me out onto the rooftop heliport, and we scramble across to the doors. A medic is waiting and begins to assess my injuries. I'm immediately put on a stretcher and wheeled away through the corridors. Everything is becoming a whirl. Nurses and a doctor are checking everything, asking me to undress and get into their ridiculous gowns that expose your rear. The curtain is closed, and I wave at Freddie as he is ushered away. I think some morphine is given to me as I drift into sleep and leave this crazy chaotic nightmare.

***

The next sensation is one of floating, like coming out of the well. That weird feeling of seeing things in a shimmy haze, when you are not sure if you are awake or dreaming. I hear voices all jumbled up and lights flashing. Am I still in the hospital or moving? I have that numb feeling of dreamland when you want to move and wake up, but you feel pinned down, unable to respond. I close my eyes (I think) and drift, my body shuffling around without any cooperation from my brain. My mouth speaks and I hear noise, but I have no idea if its real. Looking to the left, I watch as someone stabs me with a needle. I try to react but overwhelming darkness crashes over me.

***

A voice echoes in my head, one I don't recognise. It agitates me and I start to writhe around, my arms feeling like octopus tentacles, dislocated and numb. I think I swiped the voice as it yelled and invisible hands clamp me down. I get some visual on the face that appeared over me. NO, it can't be! Chase is dead, *what*?? My heart rate races, and panic grips my chest. I see her throat ripped and blood pouring out of it. I scream and cry out. Then another needle is pushed into my arm. The face disappears into a tunnel as I yell *NO, NO* in my head.

***

Warmth.

Light.

Tightness holding me still.

Am I awake? I blink and focus on the nearest thing. It's a flower vase, with a colourful bouquet. Over my head is a white boom with a monitor and other things dangling. I strain my neck to look around this room. It's a hospital bed, in a private room, as I'm the only one in here. The window is near allowing me to be bathed in morning sunlight; at least I think its morning. I have no watch on and there's no clock in the room. Strength slowly returns to my arms and body, as I try to prop myself up but fail and crash into the soft pillow, a pull on my arm confirming a drip is attached.

Where am I? Birds twitter away as if they are responding to me awakening and I gaze wearily through the sash window. Coming into view is a white building, the outline broken up with trees. My head is so heavy, I return to staring at the ceiling. The memory of seeing Chase invades my thoughts and I shiver, wondering if she did survive. Surely not. There was enough blood coming out of her to fill a bath. I must have been delirious, the shock still haunting me. I tense up as hear a door swish open. I glance across and see a person in a white coat pushing a trolley. It's a woman with brown hair tied up in a bun and she smiles at me.

"Maisie, so glad you are awake. It must be strange to wake up somewhere new and unfamiliar. My name is

Doctor Smith," she says with a gentle voice. Although, I naturally wonder if that *is* her real name. *Smith.* Hmm…

"You are probably wondering where you are and what has happened to you." *Yes, it had crossed my mind.* "You were brought here by helicopter and because you had sustained so many injuries from glass and intrusions you underwent surgery. This is a private hospital. It was decided to bring you here for safety and recovery reasons. We will be watching over you whilst you get well. The drip is to rehydrate you. So, I'll just do some checks, and take it out to make you more comfortable," she says as she clamps a reader on my finger and rests her hand on my forehead. I force a weak smile.

"Thanks. Where is the hospital? You don't sound French," I ask, as I'm puzzled as to what is going on.

"It is in grounds of the British security services, so you are safe here." I frown wondering why I have been brought here and not a regular hospital. She continues with her checks and seems satisfied enough to pull out the drip. The canular stings as she withdraws it. She sticks a plaster over the hole and presents me with a small tub of tablets.

"You will be on a course of antibiotics for the next week so make sure you take them to give your body the best chance of recovery." I nod. I need to get back to full strength as soon as possible. The doctor places a jug of fresh water along with a small box.

"What's that?" I ask.

"Oh, I was instructed to give it to you, by some relative I think," she responds cheerfully. "Now, if you need anything there is a button next to your bed and someone will attend. Food will be coming soon as its breakfast time," she says.

Turning, Doctor Smith recommends that I be careful as I have fresh stitches in my face and arms, along with patches on any skin that got lacerated. My thinking starts to go into overdrive.

"Oh, before you go…what happened to Olga, Olga Gabrys. Is she ok?" The doctor gives me a puzzled look.

"I don't know of anyone with that name I'm afraid. Is it a relative?" I nod, wondering why she doesn't know about her.

"Also, Frederick Halbert, is he ok?" Again, she looks clueless.

"No one of that name here," she replies. I feel a panic rising. Where are they? Why have I been separated from them?

"Ok…thanks," I say, feeling abandoned. The doctor trips through the door and silence closes in on me. I think the tablets must drugging my senses as I uncontrollably drift off again.

32 - The Agent

A chink of plates and glass wake me, the smell of hot food licking at my senses. My weary eyes make out steam rising from a plate on the table next to me. Someone stands with it as if on guard. She smiles and pours a glass of water.

"Your breakfast Maisie. We thought you would be in the mood for some sustenance. A cooked breakfast is what you requested, so I hope it's to your liking," she says. *I asked for it?* I don't remember asking for anything.

"Ok...thanks," I say as I prop myself on painful elbows.

The cuts are everywhere, as I look around my arms. Gauze covers them, making me look like an Egyptian mummy. She turns to leave and reminds me to use the buzzer if I need anything else. I look at the food and wonder if my stomach can keep that down. I take the water and gulp. The cold revives my senses and I take a better look out of the window. It appears to open out onto a courtyard, still bathed in sunlight. I see people in white smocks wandering between buildings, odd ones holding electronic pads. I wonder what sort of facility this is. Does it mean I am no longer in France?

The food beckons me, so I carefully take a mouthful. Even chewing is challenging work. Everything is hurting. As with all things, persistence helps, and I begin to enjoy it and feel better. The breakfast *is* to my liking, even though I'm not sure how I requested it as I was drugged at the time.

The parade of white coated people continues while I gaze onto the sunlit courtyard. I'm hoping that someone can give me answers soon. I can feel my impatience rising. *Must be getting stronger*. Another woman comes to take away my dishes and asks if tea or any other drink would suit. I ask for the usual, hoping that isn't off the menu. She nods and reassures me that some will appear.

Gingerly, I try to get up and go to the loo, as the water is forcing a reaction from me, along with all the drugs with which I've been pumped. My legs have numerous bruises and lacerations. I thought the suit would have protected me more. Anyway, it's all a bit uncomfortable this moving around, so I carefully return to sit in a chair and continue my people watching. Where is Olga and Freddie? And why am I here? Is this in France or Britain? So many questions, my head is hurting. The door creaks open, and a woman dressed in a black suit walks efficiently towards me.

"Good morning, Maisie. I trust you are beginning to feel more like yourself. My name is Ayanna Bolt. I work for MI6. You are probably wondering why you are here," she says, with a West Indian lilt. I nod. "For your own safety, we brought you here after the, shall we say, interesting episode in Versailles. Our counterparts in France notified us that you were needing a lot of care, and to save any embarrassment to their authorities, we acted to extract you." She sits on the edge of the bed.

"Oh, I see," I say, feeling the weight of the world on me.

I caused so much destruction to a national treasure along with injuring and killing someone, I suppose it would pose a few questions. She continues to gaze at me.

"You are so young. How did you get involved in this business? We know from our records that your parents died in service years ago. It was thought you were lost too. And now, you appear in an international brawl. Where have you been all these years?"

I see her disbelief is seeking some answers. I'm not sure what I should tell her. Is she trustworthy? I shrug my shoulders and create a pained face. She smiles, either, understanding I am in pain or trying to misdirect her.

"I know you are still recovering from the shock and the surgery, so these questions can wait. We will have more time to discuss this when you are fit enough to visit." *Visit where?* "I think you will be resting for some time, so make the most of it." She starts to get up, so I raise my arm. Ow, that was unwise.

"I have a few questions myself." She stops and looks sympathetically at me. "What happened to Olga Gabrys? She was taken to a hospital for surgery I think." Ayanna purses her lips and gives me a sideways look. "Also, there was a boy, well a man, Frederick Halbert. Is he ok?" I try to stop a tear forming.

"Olga Gabrys is wanted by MI6 for espionage and murder. She was in a French hospital but mysteriously disappeared. We were on the way to ensure she was extradited but we were too late." She gives me a concerned look. "Why do you ask about her? Do you know anything that could help us?" I tense up, wondering what I *should* say. She was not in good physical health after the shooting.

"I wish I could, but I have no idea. She was in the room when all hell broke loose and people were dying around me," I say innocently. I'm not sure if she buys this or not, as her brow keeps furrowing.

"As for Frederick Halbert, I believe he is under diplomatic restriction, his father being a diplomat. As far as I know he is well, but no more than that. Anyway, take the time to rest and we can talk later."

She again starts to make her way to the door. A quick glance back and smile gives me a little reassurance that she is for me.

I wonder who took Olga and where? Did the agency extract her? And as for Freddie, he's probably grounded for life, getting involved in all this crap. Will I ever see him again? I turn to the window and allow a pent-up tear to roll.

I glance at the box on my table and carefully reach across. Who sent me this? I open it, expecting something to spring up. Inside there is a watch and a small device. Looks like what I keep my tracks on. Great, I can have some music to sooth my troubles. I put the ear pods in and press the button. It's not what I expected.

"Maisie. You are under MI6 guard in a private hospital in London. Your surgery went well and I'm sure you will recover. It is with regret I must inform you that due to agency and other organisations infiltrating my data, I am compromised. I have undertaken a lengthy self-clean operation to remove any virus which leaves me open to hackers. This is my last notification to you. Stay well and safe.

Your next decisions will be crucial to your future. As you are aware, MI6 served your parents well and can direct you too. However, you will have to choose wisely who you associate with. When I am clear I shall contact you again. Your parents would be proud. This message will now be erased."

Wow. I almost feel sorry that Anton won't be online. He has managed to protect me through all of this, so I will miss his annoying interference. I now hear music filtering through. He must have compiled my play list, as hear Caitlyn Scarlett and others I love. What a star! I lean back in my window seat and soak in the increasing warmth and let me my mind drift again, allowing the drugs to do their healing work.

33 - The New Job

It has been almost fifteen days locked up in this room and it's driving me crazy. I've been allowed to do one or two circuits of the forecourt outside my window under strict guard, and a little weight training. I feel so much stronger, and my wounds are healing well. They have taken off my bandages and dressings, along with half of the stitches.

Those in my face were painful, like slowly drawing a rope through my cheek. The nurse who did it was in danger of being hit as it made me tense up. I gave her such a stare she was reluctant to continue. Doc Smith though, persisted and said it would only heal with minimal scarring if I was compliant. Ha…when have *I* been compliant?

Agent Ayanna Bolt has arrived to take me to wherever she wants. There are two other guys with her who are ready to escort me. I am always twitchy when this sort of situation happens as I feel hemmed in. I was persuaded to give a debrief with MI6, so they have all the details of my involvement in 'Versailles gate'.

Ayanna has consistently told me that I am not being held as a prisoner but under protective guard. They have intel that would indicate that agencies are wanting me out of the way – permanently. I can see this has exasperated Ayanna as she is desperate to get information out of me. I know she is wanting to help, but I am reluctant to divulge anything that would comprise Anton and my parents' legacy.

The black sedan waits gently purring outside the hospital. It's a huge relief to be on the other side of that building. To see the road alive with people and traffic makes my heart flutter. *Freedom.* I get in the car, with Ayanna and one guy in the back, the other in the front. The guy sat next to me has barely eye-balled me, so I wonder if he even knows I'm here. Ayanna chats away as usual, explaining where and what will happen next.

"We are now going to HQ and will meet up with a psychologist and another colleague who will debrief you," she says. I'm going to see a *shrink!* It will be interesting what they make of me.

"Don't be worried; they are professionals with the intention of ensuring you are ok. You may have been traumatised by all of this and we are checking you out." I nod. What does she mean by that?

We pull into an underground carpark and exit into a lift. The two guys have not spoken a word, so I can't help but force something. I step on the foot of one, and 'accidentally' elbow the other. They both give a quiet yelp and adjust my position, as if arranging a mischievous child, returning to their stoic staring.

Ayanna smiles and jostles me along the corridor. The building we are in must be the MI6 HQ as I come to a desk with a clerk. He gives me a lanyard saying 'Guest,' with the SIS logo on it. *That for the ignorant means 'Secret Intelligence Service'.* I am now officially in the building my parents would have known so well over the years. A well of pride and emotion builds up. I wonder where they would have sat, worked, chatted. The offices are open and arranged like I would imagine they would be. Screens and tables in huddled together I presume for different teams.

We pass by these and head for a room which opens out with a view over the River Thames. I'm starting to feel tense, like I'm going to the dentist. Two people introduce themselves as Prof Longstaff and Agent Sinclair. Ayanna sits down dismissing the two heavies.

"Maisie Greene – it is a pleasure and a surprise that we meet. I was an associate of your parents many years ago," says the Prof. She gives a warm smile and sits down beside Ayanna. Sinclair sits to one side, operating recording equipment.

"How old are you now?" the Prof asks.

"Seventeen - as far as I know," I reply. The drugs have left my mouth dry, and I give a hacking cough. The agent brings over a jug of water and glass. I nod.

"My God, which means it's over twelve years ago since I worked with them. Also, I am so sorry for your loss. Did you know about your parents and their involvement with MI6?" she asks. I tell her that it was only a recent revelation.

"Now," she continues, "this meeting is to establish what you know about their work and why you engaged in the unfortunate incident at Versailles. I am guessing it will be complicated, but we are only here to help you. We owe it to your parents as much as anyone. Those of us who knew them, dearly miss them." She gives me a calm look, one that is well versed in drawing out the depths of one's soul. I can feel myself squirming already.

***

We take over three hours, chatting and eating lunch and describing the Hall of Mirrors and Harmony Chase and the strange man with no name. The Prof seems happy with what I have divulged, with me trying to keep Olga out of it as far as I can.

Why I am feeling so protective of her, I do not know. I should be hanging her out to dry, but a weird sort of loyalty is controlling my mind. The sapphire and its information are the largest concern for them, as they suspect what it contains but have never been able to find it. Now it is out in the open market, they are urgent about tracking it and shutting it down. Ayanna adds her own observations.

"Maisie, it is obvious to me that you are holding some things back. I know it is difficult to break free from your old life, one of reliance on this clandestine agency. But your experience and knowledge would be invaluable to us if you would consider helping us," she says smiling.

I think carefully as to what I *should* say, as it might incriminate me, being Olga's assistant all these years.

"Look; I'm just a kid who wants to live a normal life. I've missed a stack of things, so you have to give me some slack *and* reassurance that you don't come on me like a tonne of bricks," I say hopefully.

The prof and Ayanna glance at each other and nod to Agent Sinclair to switch off the recording.

"Ok Maisie, we want to know all that you know. It's going to be a long process and I appreciate you must be in shock, so we are happy to be patient. Also, let me reassure you that everything you tell us is confidential and you face no repercussions. Agent Bolt and I will make sure our superiors will accept responsibility for you. So, thank you for what you told us so far. We will end todays debriefing and show you to your quarters." *Oh, I'm staying here too, am I?*

Ayanna leads me out into another section of the building. I have little clothing and no personal stuff. I did wonder what happened to all my gear, with all this moving around. It's probably being analysed by some greasy haired lab assistant. I saunter behind her and can't help thinking about the way forward. Should I give them all the dross on the agency? What would I get in return? She points to a room and leads me into a single bedded flat. It has a bathroom and small kitchen area, looking out towards the railway and a green area beyond.

"Here we are. A place to chill out for the time being. I'll show you where the canteen is and get you a pass card for areas that you can go. Obviously, some parts are out of bounds. There is a gym if you want one and a swimming pool. You will need some clothes and personal stuff, so we could go out and do some shopping if you like," she says. "Gives me something else to do, instead of wandering these corridors!"

She smiles. I think Ayanna is someone I could rely on. I study her braided hair and those sparkling dark eyes. She must be in her early twenties. A tingle goes up my back as I get a sister feeling about her.

"Great," I say with some relief. I am desperate to get my shit sorted out. "When can we go?" She tells me she is busy for the rest of the day, but this evening we could go out and get a few things.

"First, we must get your pass sorted. So, come with me and we will make you more than just a guest." We wander down to a reception desk and she asks for me to be registered. The man looks up and asks my name. I feel a tingle rising. This is the moment I've been waiting for…

"G… *Maisie G.*"

Acknowledgements

As always with writing, the nearest and dearest are the ones who should have the most thanks! They are the ones who are deprived of your presence for hours, if not days, in the pursuit of excellence. So, thanks to you family and friends who have forgotten what I look like and the sound of my voice!

I would like to thank David for his unwavering correcting of my grammatical and contextual mishaps. Mish Piri, the artist who has done a marvellous job on the cover art. Thank you to Dave and Esther, who had the foresight to encourage me to get on with writing and turn it into published works.

I would like to thank those of my readers who have bought and read and given me honest feedback. You are a treasure!

I want to thank all the great writers who imagined the spy thrillers which I have grown to love over the years and sparked the idea that I could one day join you in creating characters and plots that were fun to read. Perhaps not such a mission impossible…

Printed in Great Britain
by Amazon